GHOSTS
AROUND THE CAMPFIRE

stories by
RON SCHWAB

Leafcutter Publishing Group, Inc.
PO Box 6105
Omaha, NE 68106

ISBN: 1-943421-08-0
ISBN-13: 978-1-943421-08-4

GHOSTS AROUND THE CAMPFIRE

Dedicated to my parents, Dr. and Mrs. C. B. Schwab,
who always cared enough to make the time.

Contents

Introduction

A GLOWING CAMPFIRE; a still, dark night—they still trigger boyhood memories of Boy Scout camping trips and assemblies at summer camp when weary young men gathered around the blazing fire at day's end to join in loud singing and watch corny skits, and finally, as the flames died down to smoky coals, to listen to an offering of some new ghost story, or, many times an old favorite.

Kids seem to want to be frightened, and after the campfire story, we usually were, looking over our shoulders uneasily as the light slowly faded away, wondering what phantoms might be lurking in the woods outside the campfire ring. The owl's soft hoot became the moan of a lost ghost; the rustling cottonwood leaves became the footsteps of some wandering vampire in search of his evening meal. We knew that the spine-tingling story was a fabrication of someone's imagination—or at least we thought so —but it added another element of adventure to our sojourn in the wilderness.

My father was a Scoutmaster, and scouting was a way of life for our family when I was growing up. In my high school and college days, I spent most of my summers working at Boy Scout camps for our local council, and the campfire program was my stock in trade, the ghost story, my special forte.

Years later, I would encounter young men I had met as boys at summer camp and few remembered that I had been the instructor who taught pioneering skills with knife and axe and rope, or later, the camp program director. But, invariably, they recalled that I was the "guy who told the scary ghost stories."

When I had children of my own, I followed in the footsteps of my father and served as Scoutmaster of a troop of rambunctious boys. I am not a particularly warm person— perhaps a bit stuffy, to tell the truth—but I think my storytelling was important to establishing whatever rapport I had with my scouts, and I take no small measure of satisfaction from the encore requests I now receive from grandchildren and their friends.

But storytelling is not for boys alone. Girl Scout campfires and school events have been my forum on many occasions.

More important, however, are the stories themselves. They are really meant for ears, not eyes, and I hope the reader will seize upon opportunities to retell them to his or her own audiences on dark, spooky nights when the spirits roam the campgrounds, or halls, or wherever they may be dwelling for the moment.

Anyone can tell a ghost story. True, some storytellers have a natural talent, an enviable flair for captivating an audience with a ghostly tale, but even a shy, soft-spoken individual can spin a spell-binding narrative upon applying a few simple techniques. Foremost is selection of a good story. Certain stories will simply not be effective when told during daylight hours, no matter how skillful the storyteller. The mood created by darkness can be all-important in those cases. Some stories will be extremely suspenseful and interesting when told around a fading campfire in the middle of dense woodlands, but the same story will fall flat when delivered in a huge meeting hall. A good example of this is "The Legend of the Hand," which appears in this book. Mood is critical to the successful telling of this story, for it demands darkness and an outdoor setting. It is especially recommended as that final bedtime story before overnight campers traipse off to their bedrolls—that is if the leader is prepared to stay up the night for those who inevitably seek out his protection when they imagine a visit from the subject of the story.

A good storyteller will also have a repertoire of stories that will enable the teller to match the tale to a particular audience. Most stories have amazing flexibility. With a change in gender here and there, addition of gory details in some instances and deletion in others, they can be adapted to almost any group.

Nonetheless, the inexperienced storyteller should make the tale selection with special care. If the audience consists of ten- and eleven-year-old boys or girls, use a short story, not more than ten minutes, or risk losing the audience to restlessness and boredom. A few of the more romantic stories in this book, although 'G-rated,' would likely not be suitable for some younger audiences. Good selection takes no great skill, only common sense, a conscious effort to relate to the persons who are going to be hearing the story.

Atmosphere is critical. A ghost story told in a brilliantly lit banquet hall is doomed to failure. Darkness is the ally of those who specialize in the stories of the supernatural. Man seems to equate darkness with death and mystery, and, of course, these are ingredients of the typical ghost story.

There is also a decided advantage to telling the story in the outdoors, perhaps in a thickly wooded glen or some other secluded place beyond the security of four solid walls. Around the campfire, a story is most intriguing when the fire is nearly burned out and there is little light remaining. If the story must be narrated inside, the lights should be dimmed, even turned off. A few well-placed candles or a kerosene lantern can contribute greatly to the eerie mood in such instances. The proper atmosphere will counteract many deficiencies in the story itself or the manner of its presentation. Given the proper environment, the imaginations of the listeners will lift a considerable burden from the narrator.

Personalization of the story will boost the credibility of the ghost. The listeners should be made to identify personally, in some way, with the story so they can see themselves as participants, or, at least, potentially so. Sometimes a storyteller can accomplish this by presenting the story in first person, as an experience that actually happened to the teller. Almost any story can be adapted to this type of narration and many persons find it easier to tell a story in this manner.

Others create identification with the story by setting it in the locale where it is being told. For instance, a Boy Scout troop happens to be camping near a lake, and the story setting is near a lake; the events in the story, of course, occurred at the very lake where the Scouts happen to be camping. This always raises the possibility that the ghostly apparitions still frequent the place and may well be encountered by one or more of the listeners before the night is over. Always be alert for ways to personalize and for methods to bring the story closer to the audience.

Dramatization always helps. A competent actor can certainly do much to enliven any narrative, especially the ghost story, but one does not need to be a card-carrying thespian in order to make a successful presentation. The most important thing is to know the story well enough to tell it in one's own words. A ghost story should not be read to the audience; it should be told. A polished performance is unnecessary and, in fact, some hesitancy, or a pregnant pause, on the part of the teller may add a touch of realism and spontaneity. Most persons have on occasion told a bedtime story to small children. A ghost story may be told in the same way, and since the story is all-important here, the typical audience will not miss the dramatic touches that might have been addressed.

Nevertheless, the ghost story offers ample opportunities for the amateur actor who wishes to embellish the tale with some sound effects at appropriate intervals. A scream in the night; the low, mournful howl of the werewolf; some whispered dialogue— these things can contribute greatly to any good story. But not all storytellers feel comfortable resorting to these techniques. Those who do need little coaching; they will know instinctively when to quicken the pace of the story, when to slow down the tempo. They will know when a change in volume will bring an audience reaction and when intense dialogue may best convey the story.

The reader should not overlook the possibility that he has the latent talent to offer a story in this manner. An aspiring storyteller should experiment and test, always seek the outer limits of his dramatic ability in an effort to create a better story.

Good reading and good story telling. May the ghosts be with you.

The Legend of the Hand

I LOVE THE Rock Creek campground with the clear stream rolling over its stone bed and creating the constant, gentle babble that lulls one to sleep even at mid-morning. I visit and picnic there as often as I can—but never at night. Not since the camping trip I made with my old scout troop when I was thirteen years old. I remember what happened that night as if it had happened yesterday.

It was a typical hot, humid, almost suffocating, July evening, and I still vividly recall the eerie stillness as we sat around the campfire. Whenever we camped, the evening campfire was a tradition, and as we would watch it burn down to a few dying embers, our Scout leader customarily related stories about the history and background of our particular camping area. One story he told at the Rock Creek site, and the events that followed left an emotional wound that never fully healed.

The tale our leader told was of a small band of Spanish Conquistadors who had wandered north from Mexico exploring this part of our country long before it was settled by the white man. Apparently, as dusk settled in at the end of another scorching July day, the wanderers happened upon the place now called the Rock Creek campground and agreed to stop for the night. As might be expected, the soldiers were sweat-soaked and bone-weary from ceaseless travel. They were irritable and hostile and few spoke as they built the fires for their skimpy meal.

Later, as the men sat in somber silence about the fires, the quiet was ended abruptly by a man called Garcia. The dark, giant of a man, with a dusty, scraggly beard, stomped boldly into the middle of the camp and roared, "My ring! My ring! Some thief has taken my gold ring!"

Then he turned and glared at a slight, beardless young Spaniard squatting alone near a small fire at one corner of the camp. A shy, soft-spoken man, Juarez tended the horses and pack animals for the band.

Garcia bellowed, "My gold ring was in the leather pouch on my horse. You are the only other man who has been near that horse and are the only one who could have stolen the ring."

In a single motion Garcia drew his gleaming Spanish sword and marched across the camp to face Juarez. The young Spaniard, too terrified to speak, bolted upright and started to flee for the horses, but was tackled and thrown to the ground by several other companions. They dragged him closer to the fire.

Garcia kicked a log toward the trembling, fear-stricken Juarez, who was pinned to the ground, and ordered, "Place his arm on the log."

No one dared question an order from Garcia, and Juarez's right arm was positioned across the log as directed. Without another word, Garcia lifted his sword, and, with a single sweep, brought it down across Juarez's arm, severing his hand from the arm at the wrist. Juarez's screams shattered the night air and sent shivers like an icy, winter wind down the backs of the on-looking

Spaniards.

Garcia stooped to pick up the severed hand, but evidently it had been lost in the turmoil of the moment. He turned to Juarez and met glassy eyes filled with hate.

Juarez's face was ghostly white from shock as blood spewed from the open wound at the end of his arm. He gasped, "Garcia, you will not live the night, and the curse of my hand shall be upon all who come to this place." He struggled to get up, reaching for Garcia with the hand that was no longer there and then he fell forward, sinking to the earth with his face landing in the fire. At that precise moment, a sharp gust of wind whistled through the camp. The surrounding trees shook and the leaves rustled and, abruptly, the stillness returned.

Juarez was dragged to a spot about fifty feet south of the camp and was buried near a small oak tree. Later, as the soldiers nervously rolled out their blankets in preparation for sleep that would surely be uneasy that night, a small golden object fell from Garcia's blanket. He stooped and picked it up. He had found his ring.

The next morning, the soldiers rose one by one to get ready for their journey. All, that is, except one. Garcia would never rise again. He was stretched out on his blanket with a look of indescribable fear frozen on his dead face, his eyes bulging from their sockets. The only signs of violence were bruises and the faintest outlines of bloody fingerprints on the flesh about his throat and neck.

The Spaniards wasted no more time and quickly readied their mounts and hastily departed from the spot, leaving Garcia to provide a meal for the black, ominous vultures that soared ever-closer from the sky above.

Our Scoutmaster said there had been recurring stories about people who claimed strange happenings at this campsite. It had even been said that others had died there from some type of strangulation, although no such stories had ever been proved or confirmed. Others were said to have seen a single glowing, fluorescent-like hand floating about the camp or in the surrounding trees at night.

Needless to say, we knew that our leader had come up with another one of his tall tales and we went to bed laughing and joking, although perhaps a bit nervously, about the legend of the hand.

Eventually, the last of the campers dropped off to sleep. I slept soundly enough until I was awakened by the low howling of a wind that suddenly swept through the camp. Then I felt a slight thumping pressure moving up my chest, as though a small animal were crawling on my blanket. Suddenly, something grabbed my throat and began to squeeze firmly. My first thought was that someone was playing a prank and I struck out. I hit nothing. The pressure became suffocatingly greater. Just as I was about to black out, I was able to choke out a coughing and rasping sound that awakened my friend in the next bedroll. He looked toward me and started screaming again and again, hysterically. The pressure suddenly eased and finally stopped.

My friend's screaming brought our Scoutmaster and other campers tumbling from their bedrolls to see what was wrong. My friend insisted that he had seen a glowing hand grasping my throat. Our leader maintained that the Scout was having a nightmare because of the campfire story. No one could explain the bloody fingerprints and bruises on my neck, however, and for some reason, our troop never camped overnight at Rock Creek again.

The Weeping Wind

THE OREGON TRAIL winds through Jefferson County, Nebraska, and in the mid-1800s many settlers passed through the area on their way west. In 1869 James and Mary Robinson and their two small children, Robert, eight, and Catherine, six, pulled their covered wagon off the trail for the night.

Shortly before sundown, Mrs. Robinson asked her children to pick mulberries from a grove of trees a short distance from the wagon. As the children approached the grove, a doe and her fawn darted across their path and, as boys will do, Robert chased after them in pursuit. Catherine skipped on to the mulberry grove and began picking the ripe berries, sampling her harvest as she slowly filled her pail. Darkness began to set in, and when Robert did not come to help, Catherine returned to the wagon with her berries, complaining to her mother that Robert had not done his share of the chore.

Several hours passed and Robert still did not return to the wagon. His parents became increasingly apprehensive when they noticed lightning in the sky northwest of their camp and heard the low rumbling of thunder that confirmed a storm would arrive before the night was out. They built up the fire and, hoping that the light would be seen by Robert, and, leaving Catherine with the wagon, the parents set out to search.

Overcome with fear for her son's safety, Mrs. Robinson wandered unthinkingly into the rolling hills southwest of the wagon, calling repeatedly, "Robert! Robert!" As the angry wind signaling the approaching thunderstorm whistled through the hills, the panic-stricken Mrs. Robinson's calls became screams and she ran and stumbled wildly over the rocky slopes moving ever further from the family camp.

In the meantime, Robert walked casually into camp with the collection of toads and snakes he had gathered during his exploration of the surrounding countryside. Mr. Robinson returned shortly thereafter just as the first drops of rain began to fall. The family called again and again for Mrs. Robinson, but she was now too far from the wagon to hear their anguished summons.

As the full force of the raging storm struck the hills, Mrs. Robinson struggled to the top of a ridge and now, some three miles from the camp, she could barely make out the flickering of the fading campfire flames. Recovering her composure momentarily, she started in the direction of the camp when a bolt of lightning flashed from the sky, striking a small tree not far from where she stood. The electrical shock ripped through her body sending her tumbling down the hill into a small ravine where she lay unconscious.

The next morning, the storm subsided and Mrs. Robinson slowly regained consciousness. All she could remember was that she was looking for her lost son, and again she began to wander aimlessly through the hills calling, "Robert! Robert!"

For more than a week, the Robinson family looked for their

wife and mother. Finally, they despaired of ever finding her, and, assuming she was dead, packed their belongings and departed to continue their journey west.

Several hours after the departure of her family, Mrs. Robinson staggered and crawled into the clearing where the family had camped. She gazed about blankly at the empty campsite, only half-conscious that this was the place that had been inhabited by her family those past days. Tears rolled slowly down her cheeks as she slipped quietly and resignedly to the ground, her back resting against a large cottonwood tree. She stared ahead with glassy eyes calling again and again, "Robert! Robert!" She never left that spot again.

Summer surrendered to fall and soon the cold snows of winter covered the remains of Mrs. Robinson. The following spring, another group of weary travelers paused at the Robinson site for the night. Discovering some shreds of clothing and the skeletal remains of some poor soul near the cottonwood tree, they dug a shallow grave and buried what was left of Mrs. Robinson where they had found her. As the last shovel of dirt was thrown upon the grave, the leaves of the cottonwood rustled softly, and it seemed that light gusts of wind were striking at the tree, but ignoring every other object in the camp. Then, seemingly from the wind, the travelers heard a voice, "Robert! Robert!" The emigrants decided not to stay the night.

As the years passed, there were other stories about the strange sounds and happenings at the campsite. Always, a voice was heard calling, "Robert! Robert!"

Some twenty years later, Robert Robinson, on his way east, returned to the place where he had last seen his beloved mother. He spent two days at the campsite, walking through the surrounding hills and reflecting upon the happy times when his family had all been together.

Near dusk on the second day, he was fishing in a stream about a mile southwest of the camp. Suddenly, he felt a strange tugging at his shoulder as though someone was trying to attract his attention. A light breeze whisked through the surrounding trees, and he heard a woman's gentle voice whispering, "Robert! Robert!" As though pulled into a trance, he followed the voice, which eventually led him to the cottonwood tree. For some unexplainable reason, he began to dig at the base of the tree with his hands. He dug almost frantically until he grasped a piece of decomposed bone. His hand sifted through the intermingled dirt and bones until he felt the cold touch of metal on his fingertips. He picked up the object and, cleaning off the dirt, instantly recognized his mother's gold wedding band. At that moment the wind shook the leaves of the cottonwood and he heard the voice whispering, "Robert! Robert!" Then all was quiet. He returned the band to its bed in the earth and covered the remains of his mother and knew a peace he had not known for years.

The next morning, Robert mounted his horse and continued his journey east. It is not known what became of Robert or his family, but to this day, it is said if you listen on a quiet summer evening in those hills, you will hear, through the rustling of leaves, the soft whisper of the grieving mother, "Robert! Robert!"

Mary Lee

ABOUT FIVE MILES south of the small town of Fairbury, Nebraska is an old, deserted stone farmhouse. It looks like a thousand of other empty farm homes scattered about rural America. Weeds and thistles have taken over the yard, any remaining windows are either cracked or broken, and the roof over the small front porch threatens to collapse with each new windstorm.

A century ago, the old house was the happy, bustling home of the Hans Schmidt family. Schmidt, a hard working German farmer, and his wife, Margaret, had lived in the home for some twenty years. All four of their children had been born in the home, and Schmidt and his wife fully intended to spend the rest of their lives there.

Schmidt's eldest daughter was seventeen-year-old Mary Lee, a tall, slender girl with long, flowing golden hair. The cheerful, carefree Mary Lee was the envy of all the neighborhood girls, and her warm smile and mischievous blue eyes had melted the heart of many a young man in the farm community. Her formal schooling complete, Mary Lee helped her mother with the many household tasks on the busy farm and with the care of her three younger brothers. It was assumed that she would soon choose one of the many eligible young German farmers in the community, marry, and commence her own household. But this was not to be.

In August, as she approached her eighteenth birthday, Mary Lee went to the county fair with several of her friends. As they wandered through the exhibits, Mary Lee noticed a tall, black-haired, obviously bored, young man taking notes on a small pad. In her open, friendly way, she walked over to the young man and queried, "What's so exciting?" Showing mild irritation at the interruption, James Longstreet turned, and his dark, brooding eyes met the laughing eyes of Mary Lee. From that moment the two were inseparable.

James was a young reporter who had been assigned the rather trivial task of reporting the progress of the county fair. A quiet, sensitive man, James was of dubious heritage, although his eyes reflected the part-Cherokee blood of his mother. He was a dreamer in a community that did not understand dreamers.

As the friendship blossomed into love, Hans Schmidt nagged and chastised his young daughter for her involvement with the young reporter. Although a basically kind man, Hans Schmidt was also a strict and stubborn one who had other hopes and plans for his daughter.

Finally, early one evening, Mary Lee announced to her parents she intended to marry James in spite of her father's protests. That night when James arrived to visit Mary Lee, he was confronted at the door by Mr. Schmidt and his shotgun. Schmidt ordered James to leave. An angry verbal exchange followed between the two men, and, in the excitement, the shotgun accidentally discharged, striking James in the chest and killing him instantly.

Hearing the explosion, Mary Lee dashed to the door to find her lover lying dead on the porch. She screamed, then abruptly stopped and moved slowly and silently to the body. Calmly, she sat down on the porch and cradled the young man's head in her lap. Grimly, she gazed at the pale white face below, and, in that same moment, her own face was transformed into a picture of deep gloom and sadness. Her father moved toward her, trying to explain that the gun had been fired accidentally, but Mary Lee did not seem to hear. Finally, she rose and, without a word, entered the house and climbed the stairs to her second-story bedroom. Her mother followed her to the room to try to console her, but the door was locked and Mary Lee refused to answer.

Later, in response to the family's call, the county sheriff and other authorities arrived at the home to investigate the accident. The sheriff insisted upon speaking with Mary Lee, but when Schmidt and the sheriff knocked on her bedroom door, she again refused to answer.

Suddenly, a shiver ran down Schmidt's spine and he was struck with an unexplainable panic. With all the strength he could muster, he rammed the door open and crashed into the room. He was met by the limp form of Mary Lee suspended from a beam, a strip of a bed sheet knotted about her neck and her feet only inches from the chair that had apparently been kicked over when she took her life.

Several weeks after the tragedy, without explanation to neighbors or friends, the Schmidt family vacated the home and community and was never heard from again.

Within the space of one year, three other families occupied the house. All three occupants had a common story. They claimed that the house was haunted and at night they could hear the soft laughter of a young woman moving about the premises.

The small daughter of the last family to live in the residence related that she rose from her bed and went to the kitchen for a drink of water one night. Leaving the kitchen she came upon the glowing, almost transparent, figures of a young man and woman standing hand in hand in the living room. The apparitions approached her and the young woman bent as if to kiss the child, but the little girl felt nothing but a light breeze passing across her face. Then the forms began to dissipate slowly until the glow was concentrated into two small balls of light which proceeded to float out the open window and into the surrounding trees. The little girl maintained she was not frightened when this took place; that, in fact, the rooms seemed filled with an atmosphere of love and peace. Upon being told of the night's happenings, the child's parents expressed disbelief at the story, but nevertheless made arrangements to move out of the house immediately.

Stories spread about the house being haunted, and although most people scoffed at the notion of any ghostly occupants, no one was willing to live there. Over the years, there have been other reports of persons claiming to have seen a spirit couple floating hand in hand over the hills surrounding the house. Many have reported seeing two balls of light glittering from inside the windows of the house, but these could be excused as being the eyes of an owl or other wild creature.

It is even said that if you listen closely on a quiet summer evening in the vicinity, you can hear the soft, contagious laughter of Mary Lee, as she and her beloved James take their nightly stroll through the hills. If you see two glowing objects in the black of night, remember, it may be just an owl; on the other hand, it may not be.

A Child's Love

A TRAGIC ACCIDENT occurred on Crystal Lake several years ago. Nancy and Bill Swanson and their seven-year-old daughter, Sue Ann, were enjoying a Sunday afternoon of boating and fishing on the lake. The Swansons were a happy couple, very much in love, and adored their dark pony-tailed Sue Ann who was always ready and enthusiastic for a family outing on the boat.

Nancy was a devoted wife and mother whose entire world revolved around her architect husband and petite, vibrant daughter. As the boat bobbed gently on the water, she remarked to no one in particular, "I don't know what I would do without those two."

Sue Ann, overhearing her mother's words, clambered to her mother's side, wrapped her arms around Nancy, and with a warm hug said, "Don't worry mommy, I'll never let you be alone."

Later that afternoon, without warning, a tornado-like storm suddenly swept through the lake area. In his frantic attempt to get the boat lakeside, Bill flooded the motor and the Swansons found themselves stranded in the middle of the lake; the storm's roar muffled their cries for help.

In a few short minutes, the wind struck like a sledge. The

boat was tossed into the air and the family cast like rag dolls into the lake. Nancy, although an excellent swimmer, could barely keep her head above the water as she was bounced in the churning waves. She could see no trace of her husband, but some thirty feet away she could see Sue Ann grasping some remnants of the boat. Summoning all of her strength, she stroked slowly and painfully toward her young daughter. She inched to within a few feet of Sue Ann, and just as the girl reached out her hand to grab her mother's, the wind hit again with tremendous force, and the waves carried Nancy further away from the wreckage. When she looked again, her daughter was gone.

The next day, the bodies of her husband and child were recovered. Bill and Sue Ann were buried side by side on a hill not far from a large elm tree in the local cemetery. For weeks after the burial, the grief-stricken Nancy made a daily pilgrimage to their graves. Sometimes she would sit by the elm for hours, gaze pensively into the sky, and think of happier days. Her life was without meaning.

One night, perhaps six months after the tragic accident, a young college professor was strolling along the lake shore not far from this very place. The sun was just setting and the full blackness of night had not yet descended. Daniel Baker was a handsome, blonde man who had also known sorrow. Although not yet thirty, he had been widowed as the result of an automobile accident that claimed the life of his wife, leaving him the sole parent of two small children, Jeffrey, five, and Elizabeth, three. The lonely English teacher often walked along the lake at night to be alone with his memories.

Pausing briefly this particular evening to look out onto the placid lake, he was jolted from his meditation by the cries of what sounded like a little girl coming from the middle of the lake. The lake was eerily calm, however, and there was not a boat in sight. Shortly, the cries became softer and gradually faded away. "It must have been a bird," he mumbled softly.

Then his head jerked as if an electric wire had been touched to the back of his neck. The shock was followed by a vision in his mind of a beautiful, raven-haired young woman. The woman was sitting peacefully under a tall tree, her eyes filled with pain and loneliness. Just as suddenly as the image had appeared, it disappeared. Daniel continued on his walk, uneasy and discomfited, haunted by the woman's image and the cries he had heard.

He returned home, relieved his babysitter, and tucked his children safely into bed. He slept little himself that night, unable to erase the image of the woman from his mind. A logical, practical man, Daniel rejected any notion of spirits or unearthly forces at work and convinced himself that his imagination had been overactive that evening.

For a full week he resisted the compulsion to take another walk along the lake. Finally, however, he surrendered to his impulses and went again to the place where he had experienced the strange occurrences a week earlier.

This time, the sky was overcast and the night unusually dark. He walked along the lakeshore, and he could hear the splashing of the waves against the rocks as the gentle breeze stirred the waters. He stopped abruptly when he again heard the cries from the lake. Suddenly, the cries stopped and beside him a voice whispered, "Please don't let my mommy be lonely anymore." He turned and saw nothing; again he felt a jolt in his neck and the vision of the black-haired woman came alive in his mind.

He struggled futilely to sleep that night, the ghostly experiences torturing him as he sought an explanation.

Late the following afternoon, leaving the University, Daniel did not drive directly home as was his custom. For some reason, which he could not explain, he drove in the opposite direction from his home with no particular destination in mind. For nearly an hour he drove aimlessly, without purpose, until he came to a small cemetery. On impulse, he turned onto the narrow, gravel road that wound through the cemetery.

Driving slowly up the sloping road, he found himself drawn to the far end near a large elm tree on top of a hill. When he reached the tree, he stopped, got out, and his eyes were drawn to two fairly recent grave sites as evidenced by mounds of dirt not yet fully covered with grass. Curious, he walked over to the graves, paused, and read the names on the small stones: William Swanson; Sue Ann Swanson. The names meant nothing to him, but he was disturbed by the fact that one of the graves was that of a small child. Finding himself strangely reluctant to leave the place, he finally pulled himself away, and in a state of melancholy and depression, drove home.

The following evening, Daniel was again drawn to the lake, but this time as he approached the place of his earlier experience, he saw a woman sitting on the soft grass near the lake shore. Drawing closer, he was shocked to recognize the woman whose image had so abruptly visited his mind on the earlier occasions. He stopped and almost turned to leave, but felt as if someone was tugging at his hand and leading him toward the woman.

When he was close enough to touch her, he said haltingly, "Excuse me. I didn't mean to intrude," and backed away.

Startled, Nancy rose to face Daniel and responded with

hesitation, "Please stay." Together they sat down.

For some moments they sat there in silence. Daniel spoke first and introduced himself. Nancy responded, "I'm Nancy Swanson." Upon hearing the name, Daniel thought of the two graves. Soon they were talking quietly and easily as if they were long-time acquaintances, sharing the tragedies and joys of their respective lives.

The following evening they met again and talked for hours, but Daniel said nothing about the strange events that seemed to conspire to bring them together. They were alone no more.

The Big Cat

THIS STORY HAS its roots in a Native American legend. According to the legend, a portion of southeastern Nebraska lying north of the Kansas line was taboo to several tribes of Native Americans. The land was said to be sacred and those who entered rarely returned to tell about it. The Native Americans claimed that the Great Spirit had designated the mountain lion as guardian of the sacred land, and that those who ventured there would meet their death at the claws of the lion. Furthermore, the spirit of those who died in this manner took on the form of the lion, and the violators of the sacred land, instead of entering the happy hunting ground, were destined to walk the earth as huge lion-like beasts.

Whether the legend has any validity or not is unknown. We do know that there were confirmed stories among the Pawnee of warriors who had traveled into the sacred land and escaped. Apparently in all instances, however, they were seriously injured and maimed by giant mountain lions. One reported being attacked by a huge lion that walked upright on its hind feet like a man.

In any event, this is one of the few areas of Nebraska where mountain lions are rarely heard and seen. Hearing one of the creatures is unforgettable. Sometimes the cries or screeching of a mountain lion at night will be mistaken for a woman screaming.

One night, a group of hunters were camped at a wooded site near the Little Blue River. Just before midnight, they were awakened by a screeching or screaming noise in the woods, and, at first, thought it was a human voice crying for help. One of the hunters, however, recognized the ungodly racket as the cry of a mountain lion, and grabbing his rifle, dashed into the woods for a shot at the animal.

Shortly, the other hunters heard the gun fire followed by the blood-curdling screaming of their companion and the roar and growling of some beast . . . then deathly silence. The remaining hunters, weapons in hands, ventured into the trees in a half-hearted attempt to find their friend. They found nothing and decided to wait until morning to search further.

At sunrise, they again scoured the surrounding area and found no sign of the lost hunter. One of the men did discover an area of matted grass and broken brush where there had obviously been a struggle. Thick, dry blood caked the grass, but there were no possessions of the hunter to evidence he had been there.

After the incident was reported to the authorities, other searchers combed the area without success, and ultimately the search was abandoned.

A year later, other hunters camping near the same spot gathered around their campfire's warm glow just before bedtime. Suddenly out of the blackness of the night came the cries of a mountain lion intermingled with a strange growling-grunting noise. The sound came closer and closer to the camp and the campers could hear the limbs and brush crackling as some creature approached. They huddled near the fire with rifles at the ready, throwing their flashlight beams to the edge of the trees. Several tossed added wood on the fire to heighten the blaze.

Abruptly, a huge creature, more than seven feet tall, burst into the clearing. It had the body of a mountain lion yet facial expressions common to the human species. It walked upright on its hind legs like a man, had long, sharp claws, and was covered with fur like a lion. The creature cocked its head to one side, moving its eyes from one man to the other as if trying to identify someone, before it let loose a grunting-coughing sound from deep in its throat, and one of the hunters reported seeing large tears rolling down the beast's cheeks. Its eyes seeming to reflect disappointment, the creature did an about-face and stomped stiffly and awkwardly back into the woods.

The men had been too shocked and astounded to shoot or make any other attack upon the invader, and they were not in the mood to pursue it that night. In the morning they found huge tracks which were later confirmed as the hind feet of some member of the cat family, although no track that large had ever been reported in the zoological community. Efforts to trail the animal were futile.

Since that time, others have reported giant tracks of a cat-like animal in the area, and many have heard the screeching and growling of mountain lions in the surrounding hills, but there have been no other sightings of the creature . . . to this time.

The Strawberry Patch

THIS STORY HAS its origins in Jefferson County, Nebraska. The tale is not entirely the writer's original creation, and several versions have circulated in the county for some years. Charles Dawson, in his book Pioneer Tales of the Oregon Trail, related one variation of the story. Although the story I heard at campfires over the years deviates somewhat from Mr. Dawson's account, I have referred to his book in reconstruction of the tale.

In the early 1870s, Jacob Schoenweiss and his wife, Rebecca, immigrated from Germany and traveled by covered wagon to Jefferson County, Nebraska, where they homesteaded a farm northwest of the town of Fairbury. The farm was bounded on the west by the Little Blue River, and on the east by the black, rich bottomland that gave way to rugged sandstone hills streaked with patches of lush native grass. A clear, spring-fed stream meandered through the small canyon near the east boundary.

The Schoenweiss family arrived in early fall and with the help of neighbors, completed a small two-room sod house just in time to defend against the icy blasts of an unusually vicious Nebraska winter.

With the arrival of spring, Jacob began breaking ground and planting crops. The family found that food sources were plentiful in the countryside. Besides ample wild game, there were gooseberries, raspberries, and other edible plants. Late in the spring, Mr. Schoenweiss was especially pleased to find that the area along the stream was covered with patches of luscious strawberries.

One bright June morning when there was a lull in the field work, Jacob and Rebecca set out hand in hand to gather a pail of wild strawberries. Strolling along the stream, they found themselves in the middle of a huge patch of giant strawberries which they began to harvest quickly. Rebecca spotted an area next to an outcropping of sandstone and shaded by scattered clumps of underbrush. She scurried to the spot and discovered the largest, thickest strawberry plants she had ever seen, all covered with enormous blood-red strawberries. She summoned her husband, and excitedly they jumped to the task of picking berries, eating some of the better ones as they harvested.

When they had nearly filled their bucket, Jacob's foot caught on a tree root, and he tumbled to the ground, falling flat on his chest. Raising himself on his hands, he found himself face to face with a human skull. Leaping to his feet, he called to his wife who, upon seeing the eyeless, naked skull grinning at her from its moss-covered abode, nearly fainted. Searching further, they discovered that underneath the strawberry foliage and half-buried in the earth were the bones and skulls of many other persons for whom the strawberry patch had evidently been the last resting place.

Finally, Jacob and Rebecca concluded their search, pausing for a moment in silence and Jacob picked up the bucket and poured the berries onto the ground. They both knew what had caused the berries to grow so big and red.

Soberly gathering the skulls and bones, they assembled the remains of what they judged would have been twelve skeletons of men, women, and children. They dug a shallow, common grave, deposited the remains, and rolled a large sandstone boulder on top to mark the site. Tired and weary, they trudged home with some sense of satisfaction that they had done their duty by giving the unfortunate beings a decent burial.

After supper the Schoenweiss family assembled on the small front porch of the house, the parents welcoming the quiet and peace that came after the eventful day. But shortly after the sun had dropped below the horizon, there came a high-pitched shriek or cry, like that of a woman or child in the depth of anguish or despair. The sound was repeated again and again coming from different locations, sometimes from the ash trees surrounding the home and other times from the hills beyond. The frightened children began to whimper and cry. Jacob entered the house, grabbed his rifle, and conducted a thorough search of the premises following the voices from point to point. Finally, he heard the fearful cries coming from near the home. He returned to find his family had retreated to the house and barred the door.

The cries of the unearthly visitor were repeated throughout the night, and the Schoenweiss family found no peace until dawn's first light. Night after night, the cries returned, but gradually the family grew accustomed to the disturbance. Neighbors who visited the home also heard the cries from time to time and joined the futile search for their source. Residents of the neighborhood came to refer to the nightly sounds as the "lost woman ghost."

Summer passed and Jacob enjoyed a bountiful autumn harvest, and the family would have been extremely happy and content if it had not been for the unsettling cries of the nightly visitor. At his wife's suggestion, Jacob consented to join his wife's brother for the winter at his home further south on the Little Blue River. During the long, bitter winter, they returned only occasionally to see if everything was all right, but never stayed overnight.

When the first signs of spring arrived, the Schoenweiss family moved back to the home. The first night of their return was celebrated by the usual performance of the unseen voice. Although the cries were annoying, since no harm ever resulted, they finally decided to accept the situation as best they could.

Strawberry time came again and this time, the entire family started out to search the hillsides and ravines for the crimson berries. Their wanderings brought them back to the burial place of the unknown dead. After spending a quiet moment at the burial place, they traipsed downstream. Later they stopped to rest, and the children splashed across the stream and commenced climbing a steep, sandstone cliff on the other side. Watching the children scale the cliff, Jacob noticed that the top was capped with a thick, overhanging ledge of brown sandstone. Dark recesses in the sandstone cliff above several protruding shelves suggested ideal havens for wild animals. Scanning the coarse walls, his eyes came to rest on a ghastly sight—the skeleton of a human being sitting in a shallow cave just off one ledge.

He darted across the stream and followed his children up the side of the cliff. Upon reaching the ledge, they found that the skeleton was obviously that of a woman huddled in a crouched, squatting position with her back against the wall of the little grotto. Jacob speculated that she had taken refuge there only to be found and killed by hostile Indians.

Tenderly, the family gathered up the bones and carried them back to the burial place where they interred them with the others. The remainder of the day was spent in search for any others that might be lying unburied on the hillsides, but all they found were a few heaps of fire-warped wagon irons and charred wood near bones of horses and oxen. Several arrowheads were collected from the piles of bones.

Near dusk, the family returned home anticipating again the cries of the unseen voice. That night, however, the voice did not come, and it was never heard again by the family or anyone else in the neighborhood.

The Lost Ring

I WAS SIXTEEN years old at the time, shy and perhaps a bit naive in comparison to some boys my age. I tended to be somewhat of a loner in those years, and I guess I have not changed all that much. I was always too much of a dreamer, given to sober introspection and fantasy, never entirely in touch with reality. As for girls, well, I liked them more than a little, especially those fair, Nordic damsels who came from the Scandinavian-settled sections of our county. I had been smitten more than once by a quick smile and a pair of sparkling, blue eyes, but I had never known a girl well enough to be truly in love—not till that brisk, September night on the rim of Swenson's Canyon.

I had obtained my driver's license not long before, and it had become my custom to drive out to the canyon about dusk two or three times a week. Usually, I would park my car on the grassy meadows that covered the plateau above the canyon, then climb up the rocky slope to a cluster of mushroom-like rock formations at the highest point of the sheer canyon walls. There I would soak in the solitude and quiet, lost in the dream world I entered whenever I came to this place.

This particular September evening, though, was cooler than

normal, and a healthy breeze nipped at my ears. The rustling of the fragile leaves of the cottonwoods that covered the canyon floor reminded me that soon autumn breezes would yank away their lives and send them floating to the earth to become part of the decaying humus, another turn in nature's cycle.

An unexplainable melancholy took hold of me as I gazed into the chasm's depths. Tears moistened my eyes, and I felt an overwhelming need to cry, though I had not done so in years. Suddenly, I was startled by a soft, velvety voice from the darkness behind me.

"Hello. May I join you?"

I jumped up and turned, surprised to see a lithe, golden-haired girl, no older than myself, emerging from the blackness. She approached slowly but without the least hesitation, like a young woman on a leisurely evening stroll. I looked about nervously for some escort or companion, but she was apparently alone. As she came closer, I noticed the milky, unblemished whiteness of her face, but I was drawn, almost hypnotically, to the cobalt blueness of her limpid eyes. All of my words choked in my throat and I remained speechless.

Then, displaying a disarming smile, she said again, "May I join you?"

Finally, I stammered, "Sure. It would be nice to have some company."

We sat on the canyon rim for some moments, neither of us speaking. Her eyes seemed focused on some distant nothingness across the chasm. I could not pull my eyes from the wheat-colored hair that whipped about her neck and shoulders as gusts of wind swept over the rim. I felt so at ease with her—like I had known her forever.

"My name's Dan Barrett," I said. "I don't think I've seen you at school. Did you just move here?"

She turned toward me, offering that open, enchanting smile again. "I'm just visiting," she said. Her eyes clouded and the smile faded momentarily, before it returned. "Yes, I'm just visiting. My name's Ellen Peterson."

"Have you been here before?" I asked.

"Oh, yes," she said, "many times. I come here every time I get back."

"I come here all the time," I said. "It's just so peaceful and quiet. It helps me to think." I pulled my nylon jacket up around my neck to ward of the chill and then was aware, for the first time, that she was wearing only a light, sleeveless blouse with her flowered peasant skirt. "You must be cold," I said. I started to unbutton my jacket. "Here, put this over your shoulders."

"No," she protested, "I'm not cold. Really, I'm not. I don't like to wear anything over my shoulders . . . but I do like gentlemen and it was nice of you to offer." She smiled again and won my heart.

We must have talked for the better part of two hours, engaging in abstract, philosophic conversation. I savored those rare moments of contact with another dreamer.

Finally, she announced, "I have to be leaving now. It's been a wonderful evening."

"That goes for me too," I said. "Will you be staying here long? Will I get to see you again?"

She answered, "I'll be here again tomorrow night. I have to look for my ring."

"Your ring? I would have helped you look if you would have said something. Did you lose it here?"

"Yes, I lost it somewhere around this very spot."

"I'll come back tomorrow night," I said. "I'll help you look for it."

"Oh, thank you," she squealed. "I'll see you tomorrow night." She bent over and brushed my cheek with her soft, moist lips, just briefly and innocently, but from that moment, I was hopelessly and eternally in love with the fair-skinned nymph.

As we rose to leave, I said, "Where's your car?"

"I don't have one."

"Well then, let me take you home or wherever you're staying." It occurred to me then that in two hours I had learned nothing about the girl, her family, or her background.

"I'm just going down the road a ways," she said. "I love to walk. Please don't worry; I'll see you tomorrow night."

"Okay," I said reluctantly, "but I wish you'd let me take you home." She scampered away and disappeared into the darkness before I could object further.

I saw Ellen again the next night, and for some time, we searched in vain for the lost ring. Again, we talked openly and without restraint, but she always deftly skirted my inquiries about her home and family. Our parting was much the same and we agreed to meet there again the next night. I promised to bring a brighter lantern, hoping that might help. Tears welled up in her round eyes when she talked about the ring, and I could see it meant a great deal to her. That was enough for me. I would do anything I could to help her find it.

That third night, I was afraid she would not come again. She was late and there was a light cloud cover, so it was pitch black when she suddenly appeared on the canyon rim.

"Hi, Dan," she said, bouncing over to me and throwing her

arms around my waist as naturally and spontaneously as if she had known me for years. Her head was tilted up so that her laughing eyes met mine, and, impulsively, I kissed her lightly on the lips—the first time I had ever kissed any girl. She pressed her fingers gently to my cheek. "That was nice, Dan," she said. "I'll always remember that; I hope you will, too."

There was an ominous finality about her remark and I was seized with a moment of panic. Turning quickly to the task at hand, she said, "I can't stay as long tonight. Can we look for the ring now?"

Obediently, I turned on my lantern and commenced what I was certain was going to be another fruitless search. As I walked along the rim, I moved perilously close to the edge of the sheer cliff. Another step or two and I could drop someone hundred feet to the canyon floor. Then I noticed a little dirt-filled crevice, narrow and wedge shaped, widening and opening as it worked its way out of the edge. I bent down and began to clean out the matter that filled the narrow end of the wedge, and, shortly, my fingers tightened around a thin, metal band. After removing it, I rubbed the ring clean against my trousers and then I turned my lantern beam on it. Yes, tarnished as it was, I could make out the letters "E. P.," one letter engraved on each side of the smeared ruby. But the class year: 1944 . . . that would have been fifty years earlier.

Perplexed, I called to Ellen, who was searching down the slope with another flashlight I had brought. "Ellen, I think I found it. But I thought you said it was your ring."

She hurried up the incline, falling to her knees several times in her eagerness to reach me. Without a word, she grabbed the ring from my hand, clutching it possessively, and moved it closer to her eyes, studying it seriously before she lifted her head again and her eyes met mine. Big tears rolled down her cheeks, and I was overwhelmed by the happiness I saw in her face.

I moved toward her to take her in my arms, but as I reached out, she turned quickly and rushed away along the canyon rim, escaping into the darkness. Somehow, I knew from that moment, I would never see her again in this life. Part of the mystery of Ellen Peterson was answered for me not long after that last night together.

One evening, as I was especially overcome with a sense of loss and despair, I approached my mother in the living room of our home and asked if she had ever heard of an Ellen Peterson.

"Yes," she said, "Ellen Peterson was a young farm girl who met a tragic death not long before my parents were married in the early 1940s—Mom knew her, I think. According to my mother, Ellen and her boyfriend had quarreled one night at Swenson's Canyon. In the course of the argument, Ellen returned her boyfriend's class ring and he, in turn, had thrown hers angrily on the ground. When she rushed to pick it up, she slipped and plummeted over the cliff's edge to the rocks below."

According to my mother, Ellen's grief-stricken boyfriend had joined the army not long after, and died a hero's death in North Africa. My mother said that Ellen was buried in the town cemetery, but for some years after the accident, people had claimed to see her wandering from time to time along the canyon's edge. It was, of course, my mother said, just a sick attempt of some people to frighten others, perhaps a conscious effort to fabricate a ghostly legend. But those stories had long since been put to rest, my mother assured me.

In these enlightened times, of course, no one believes in

ghosts. Certainly I do not . . . but I do believe in Ellen Peterson.

The House That Wasn't

A MOURNFUL, GHOSTLIKE wail came out of the blackness from the far north end of the canyon, sending icy shivers down my spine. The sun had fallen behind the chasm rim less than an hour before, but in the last ten minutes a gloomy, gray cloud cover had suddenly moved in and obscured the twinkling stars that had earlier illuminated the canyon floor.

I was bone-weary after hiking and photographing the natural wonders of the Vulture Hills area for the previous three days. It was late fall in the southern Rocky Mountain foothills, but the balmy Indian summer days had lured me into a false sense of security, and I had wandered too many miles from my jeep. When the wind howled again and its frigid blasts suddenly gouged my cheeks, I knew I was in trouble.

The canyon floor could be transformed into a death trap that night, and, in near panic, I gathered my gear and started my ascent up the narrow, winding trail that led to the rocky rim some two hundred feet above. By the time I reached the top, white webs of snow were filling the chinks and crevices in the rocky terrain. I had left my parka in the jeep and had only a lightweight jacket for protection from the onslaught of the approaching storm, and I chastised myself for the sheer stupidity that led me, in pursuit of my amateur photography, to such desperate circumstances.

I had wandered the area for several days without observing any sign of human habitation, but still from my viewpoint of the rim, I searched the surrounding slopes and knolls for some sign of human life, some haven from the life-threatening storm.

Suddenly, through the milky haze, I spotted the faint orange glow of tiny lights, evidently emanating from the windows of a dwelling nestled in a hillside not more than a mile away. I could hardly believe I had failed to come across the structure as I crisscrossed the area in pursuit of subjects to photograph. But I did not wait to contemplate the strangeness of it all and immediately headed for the lights.

It was nearly an hour later when I approached the white frame house. I had been whip-sawed to exhaustion by the unrelenting wind, and as the snow deepened on the trail, my legs had become heavier until I thought I could not lift my feet to take another step. Smoke curled skyward from the small one-story home that hugged the hillside so cozily, and the thought of the warmth that no doubt lay within spurred me onward until, shortly, I stepped onto the sturdy wooden porch. Frantically, I hammered against the door and when it finally gave way, I was aware of the numbness overtaking my limbs as I fell forward and lapsed into blackness.

When I regained consciousness, my first awareness was of the life-giving heat that came from the crackling fireplace nearby. I was stretched out on the soft, carpeted floor near the hearth, wrapped like a mummy in a heavy wool blanket. When I looked up, I met the eyes of a dark-eyed young woman, perhaps nineteen or twenty years old, a few years younger than myself. The smooth, olive skin that covered high cheekbones and the shiny black hair that cascaded to the middle of her back told me Indian blood flowed in her veins. She was an exotic beauty, serenely poised.

Smiling reassuringly, she said, "You will be all right soon. Would you like some coffee?"

I nodded my head affirmatively, unable to speak, so entranced was I by the lovely creature.

When she moved away to fetch the coffee, another voice broke the silence. "You and I share some good luck, friend."

I sat up and turned my head to meet a ruddy-faced, sandy-haired young man about my age seated comfortably across the room in an overstuffed chair. "My name's Tom Riley," he said. "I was deer hunting a few miles south of here before the storm hit. If I hadn't come upon this place, I think I'd be a goner right now; I'd say the same goes for you."

"Jack Edwards," I answered. "You're right. I'm afraid I didn't show good sense wandering out there like this." I pointed to my camera resting on a coffee table nearby. "I'm a different kind of hunter . . . an amateur photographer."

"Well," Riley said, "my guess is we're going to be here a few days, and you'll probably get to do more hunting with your camera than I will with my rifle."

"Who's the girl?" I asked.

"She says her name's Anita Joliet. Apparently her father's dead and she lives here with her mother." He pointed to a closed door off the living room. "Says her mother's in that bedroom sick."

Abruptly, the young woman returned with a steaming cup of black coffee. A few gulps of the hot, black liquid, and my recovery was nearly complete.

The remainder of the evening was spent with Anita and Riley near the fire. I found that Anita was a bright, articulate young woman, knowledgeable on a number of subjects and apparently well educated, although rather secretive. Once, in the course of our conversation I asked her, "Can we be of some help with your mother? Wouldn't she be warmer out here by the fireplace?"

She smiled benignly and answered, "No. She prefers to be left to herself. She rarely leaves the room."

I shrugged in acceptance of her statement, but I thought it strange that Anita had not left the room to check on her mother during the entire evening.

That night, Riley and I bedded down on the living room floor and Anita removed herself to what was apparently another bedroom at the other end of the house just off the small kitchen area. Again, I thought it odd that she did not inquire into her mother's condition before she went to bed.

Riley and I stayed in the house for three days and they were among the most peaceful, carefree days of my life. Anita evidently had more than ample food supplies and she fed us like royalty. The three of us became fast friends, and after considerable coaxing and chiding, I convinced Anita to permit me to photograph her face. It had to be the most photogenic face I have ever seen—a photographer's dream. I captured her every mood: jubilant, pensive, sad. By the evening of the third day, I was convinced I had fallen in love.

During the day the storm had subsided and the hills were peaceful again, shrouded with the clean, white blanket of new snow. Riley and I agreed that we would depart the next morning.

That night I told Anita "Riley and I will be leaving in the morning, but I will come back soon. May I bring some supplies?"

Her face turned sad, and her lips trembled slightly as she said, "You must not come back . . . ever."

Riley was in the kitchen and I replied softly, "But I had the feeling that maybe you would enjoy seeing me again. I know I want to see you."

"It cannot be," she said. "Do not come back."

"Does it have something to do with your mother?" I asked. "Let me see her . . . maybe I can help."

Her face paled and traces of moisture came to her eyes. "No, please. You cannot."

"All right," I said, "but I will be back. That's a promise."

Later that night, I was awakened when I heard an agonizing moan from Riley's position not more than ten feet away. I looked over and saw a tiny, stooped figure bent over Riley's prone form and I sat upright. "What's the matter?" I said, assuming it was Anita.

The form turned, and I saw it had no eyes, only empty sockets emitting glaring rays of light. It walked towards me, moving into the firelight, and I realized it was a wizened, old Indian woman, crouched like a wild animal moving in on its prey. Then my eyes fastened on the gleaming, red-stained butcher knife in her right hand, and I was seized momentarily by uncontrollable terror.

"Mother!" Anita's voice called out from behind me. "No. He is only my friend. I will not leave you; I will never leave you."

The old woman was oblivious to Anita's cry and charged at me, waving the knife wildly, raking my shoulder with its keen edge as I ducked away. Before I could get to my feet, Anita had moved in on the old woman and was locked in a struggle for the knife. I lunged for the woman's arm, but could not reach it before the blade plunged into Anita's stomach. She stumbled backward into the fireplace, scattering red-hot embers onto the floor as she fell.

Instantly, the old woman dropped the knife and rushed to Anita, wailing some unintelligible, mournful chant. Suddenly, Anita and the old woman were engulfed in flames; I backed away seeing that they were beyond help. I hurried over to Riley. He was dead, his throat slit from ear to ear.

Snatching up Riley's coat, my camera and other personal effects immediately at hand, I rushed out the door and moved away from the house as it was consumed by flames.

It took me the remainder of the night and part of the next morning to make my way back to the jeep. I drove to the county seat and reported my experience to a disbelieving sheriff. He was a kindly old gentleman, but he said, "Son, there aren't any houses up there. There haven't been any up in that country for years."

"Please, Sheriff," I said, "just come with me. I'll show you. I've got some film, too, that will prove it to you later."

Reluctantly, the sheriff drove me back to the hills. With his four-wheel drive truck we were able to get closer to the site of the house. The warmth of the afternoon sun made the remainder of the journey easier going, and in a matter of a few hours, we returned to the hillside I had left the night before.

But there was no fire, no smoldering embers, only a few scattered, snow-covered boards and the remnants of a crumbling brick foundation.

"This is the old Joliet homestead," the sheriff said. "The place burned down twenty-five years ago."

"But the house was here last night," I protested. "I met a young woman here. Anita Joliet . . . that was her name."

"There was an Anita Joliet," the sheriff answered. "She lived here with her mother years ago. Her father was a Frenchman who married a Sioux woman. After the old man died, the daughter came home from college to stay with her mother. They say the old mother was crazy with fear that her daughter would leave. The daughter had a boyfriend who wanted to marry her, and the story is he came to the house one night for a confrontation with the old woman. Nobody knows exactly what happened, but the house burned down with the three of them in it. But Anita Joliet wasn't here last night. You can bet your boots on that, son."

"I'll have some film that says otherwise. I can't explain what happened to the house, but I've got some proof the girl was here."

The old sheriff shook his head and we started to walk away from the house when I saw an object amidst the snow and rubble some distance away from the old foundation.

"Sheriff . . . over there," I said. He followed me to the frozen heap. "This is Tom Riley, the man I was talking about . . . the one who was with me in the house." We looked down at the grotesque frozen corpse of Tom Riley.

That evening, under the watchful eyes of the sheriff, I developed my film, fully expecting to provide evidence that would support my version of Tom Riley's demise. My effort was futile. The film was blank. Then I remembered: they say you cannot photograph a ghost.

The Interrupted Sleep

IT WAS NEARLY ten years ago when a group of Scouts camping near Brawner Creek had an experience they will never forget. As darkness settled on the clearing, it seems that three or four of the boys sneaked away from camp with the idea that they were going to circle around the campsite and move up into the hills behind the camp. There they intended to let forth with some howling and other eerie noises for the devious purpose of frightening some of the greenhorn campers.

As they made their way up the steep hillside, one of the boys caught sight of a cave-like opening in an outcropping of sandstone not far off the trail. There are few boys who are not excited about the prospects of checking out a cave, and, in a few moments, the Scouts scrambled up a ledge that formed the porch-like entrance into the opening.

Shining their flashlights into the cave, they could see that it was not more than twelve or fifteen feet in depth and high enough that they could enter by stooping only slightly. As they peered in nervously, one of the flashlight beams came to rest on a rotting crate-like box at the far end of the cavern. Several of the boys were ready to leave at the sight of the box, but their more venturesome leader goaded them into remaining to investigate their discovery.

When they stepped cautiously into the cave they were greeted by a hideous flapping and screeching, and they fell to the floor as they were engulfed by swarms of furry bats frantically escaping through the cave's entrance. When it was quiet again, they rose, unharmed but scared half to death. Their leader, undaunted, moved toward the wooden box with his terrified companions crowding in close behind. Only when they were near enough to touch it did they realize they had come upon an old, decaying coffin.

They debated the merits of strategic retreat, until the sound of some the bats returning startled one boy so much that he stumbled and fell backward over the coffin. When he crashed against the old pine box, it splintered and crumbled like dry clay before their eyes, exposing the white corpse of the man who had been encased within. Dressed in black with sharp, angular features and dark, slicked-back hair, the corpse fit every boy's vision of the classic vampire. In any event, they did not wait to become better acquainted with the occupant of the cave. This time, their fearless leader led the boys out of the cave, down the hillside, and toward the sanctuary of their camp and the welcome light of its fires.

Upon reaching the camp, they breathlessly related their experience to the Scoutmaster who, unsuccessfully, tried to convince the boys they were victims of their own imaginations. In the morning, he said, they would all go to the cave and he would put their fears to rest.

The Scouts slept restlessly that night and there were plenty of volunteers to keep the fire going. Several times high-pitched, awful screaming echoed through the hills, and even the outdoor-wise Scoutmaster was unable to identify the sound.

Shortly after sunrise, the boys led the Scoutmaster back to the cave. On the slope below the entrance, one of the Scouts spotted a young doe stretched out on the grass. Gathering around the animal, they could see she had been dead only a short time, for rigor mortis had not yet set in. There were no signs of violence on the poor creature, with the exception of two puncture-like marks on her jugular vein, and a small smearing of blood around the tiny holes. The Scoutmaster's face turned pale and he said nothing, but the boys could sense that he was shaken and less confident now.

When they finally reached the cave's entrance, they found the cavern empty. The remnants of the coffin were evident on the floor at the rear of the cave, but the body was gone. They agreed no further examination was necessary.

After they returned to camp, the Scoutmaster admonished the boys not to speculate on the cause of the doe's death. He pointed out that a rattlesnake or a mountain lion, or any number of wild creatures, could have made the marks on the animal's neck, and he chided the boys for permitting their imaginations to run away with them. Nonetheless, the Scoutmaster did not bring his troop back to camp at any of the sites along this stream again.

Ever since that night, there have been recurring stories of mysterious animal deaths in this area. Most cases have been reported by farmers who have lost a calf or a lamb to some type of wild animal or creature that drains its victim of its blood and leaves the remainder of the carcass untouched. Investigations by the sheriff's department and health authorities have never uncovered an explanation of the deaths. So far, there have been no reports of any attacks on humans.

Whether the incidents have anything to do with what the boys claimed they saw in the cave that night, no one can say.

Girl Possessed

CINDY RANDEAU'S HYSTERICAL screaming brought the camp to life. Some of the other girls shrieked and others squirmed deeper into the security of their sleeping bags. Julie Wilson, the girls' attractive, young Scout leader, scurried to Cindy's side.

"Cindy! What is it?" she asked.

Cindy, a rather fragile-looking girl of thirteen was sitting upright on top of her sleeping bag, staring with wide, glazed eyes into the blackness of the surrounding woods, apparently oblivious to Julie's inquiry. Beads of sweat dotted her cheeks and forehead although the mid-August night was unusually cool. The girl had all of the classic symptoms of shock, Julie noted, instinctively placing her hand on the petite girl's clammy forehead.

"Cindy, are you sick?" Julie asked. "Don't you feel well?"

Cindy, her lips trembling, but uttering no sound, continued to stare silently as though some scene invisible to everyone else was unfolding on the fringes of the camp. Most of the other girls were gathered around Cindy and Julie now, gaping with fear and puzzlement at their friend.

Suddenly, Cindy began to speak—or at least a voice came

from her lips . . . a voice unrecognizable to Julie and the girls. "I have to get help for Cathy," the voice said. "She's bleeding terribly . . . and Ralph, he's unconscious, and hurt badly, too. We have to get to them . . . now!"

It was the voice of a mature woman with a rather low, almost mellow tone, in sharp contrast to Cindy's normally high-pitched voice. The words were precisely articulated, again absent of Cindy's youthful mumbling and contractions.

Julie grasped Cindy's shoulders and shook her roughly. "Cindy, wake up! You're having a nightmare. Wake up! Do you hear me?"

"I am going to help Cathy," Cindy said determinedly in the strange voice. She rose slowly and started walking toward the woods.

Julie grabbed her wrists and pulled her back momentarily. Cindy resisted with the force of a much stronger person. Julie, realizing she could not stop the girl, said, "Wait, Cindy, let me get your coat. I'll go with you."

Cindy paused and turned to Julie, her eyes acknowledging the latter's presence for the first time. "My name is Ruth," she said. "Ruth Weston. Yes, please come with me. I need your help." Tears streamed down the girl's cheeks.

Julie whirled to the other girls who were terrified and awe-stricken now, speechless, every one of them, for the first time Julie could recall. "Susan, get Cindy's jacket will you? And mine, too. It's rolled up on my sleeping bag." The wide-eyed girl nodded her head uncertainly and dashed away.

Singling out one of the older girls, Julie said, "Anne, I'm going with Cindy. I don't know what this is all about, but we can't hold her here. You're in charge while I'm gone. If I'm not back by sunrise, you send someone to the farmhouse down the road for help."

Anne, a tall, slender girl of sixteen, anxiously brushed back her short, honey-colored hair. "I'll do the best I can, Julie, but the girls are all scared to death. Do you think you should go out there?"

"I don't think I have any choice," Julie said. "There's something going on here we can't even begin to comprehend, but I have to go with Cindy. You'll be all right . . . I promise . . . and I'm counting on you, Anne. Okay?"

"Okay," Anne said. Turning to the others, she commanded, "Let's build up the fires girls, and move your sleeping bags in close. We'll stay together till Julie gets back."

Satisfied that Anne had command of the situation, Julie helped Cindy slip her jacket on over her flannel pajamas and then pulled on her own. "All right, Ruth, where are we going?"

Cindy responded in the woman's voice, "This way. Follow me."

The girl seemed to know exactly where she was going and Julie followed her obediently into the timber. They walked silently for nearly an hour until they approached a small creek that twisted and meandered its way out of the rolling foothills to the north. Julie was astonished at the girl's stamina; Cindy was not one of the stronger girls in Julie's troop, and, ordinarily, would have tired by this time. Even Julie, trim and in excellent condition, was ready for a rest after the brisk pace over the rugged countryside.

"Cindy . . . uh, Ruth, let's rest a moment."

The girl turned around and Julie saw the urgency in her face. "Please," Cindy said, in the woman's voice. "We must hurry. It will take another hour to get there and there's not much time."

Unexplainably, a shiver danced down Julie's spine. "All right, Ruth, whatever you say."

With Cindy leading the way, they headed into the hills, following the course of the creek into a rough, uninhabited area Julie had never hiked before. As they moved deeper into the hills, Cindy quickened her pace and soon began to trot ahead, like a hunting dog that had picked up a scent. It was evident they had to be near their destination . . . whatever that was.

Shortly, the fiery-orange rays of the morning sun crept over the hilltop not far ahead, and Julie caught sight of thick, black smoke curling ominously skyward against pale sky. Cindy raced toward the smoke, and Julie, seized by a new burst of energy, dashed after her. As Julie rushed over the crest of the hill, she saw the smoldering remnants of a light plane and, off to one side, Cindy kneeling at the side of a moaning child.

"Over here, quickly," Cindy called. "You have to help her; she's bleeding to death!"

Julie ran down the slope, and, as she reached Cindy, her eyes were drawn to the white, silent form beside her—a little girl with golden locks matted to her dirt-smudged cheeks.

"Her leg," Cindy said. "We have to stop the bleeding."

Julie's trained eyes appraised the compound fracture with the splintered bone piercing through the skin. A severed artery slowly pumped scarlet fluid from the little girl's body, draining it of its remaining life.

Julie knelt and ripped away part of the little girl's blouse, quickly tying the strip of cloth above the pulsating wound, tightening it with a stick until the blood flow ebbed.

"I can't leave this on long," she said, "but this will stop the bleeding until we can get something applied directly to the wound." She felt the little girl's head and took her pulse. "She's still alive ... terribly weak ... but I think she'll make it."

"Thank God," Cindy said. "And you . . . I can't thank you enough.

Then she pointed further down the slope, where Julie caught sight of two other figures sprawled on the ground: a man and a woman. She moved down the rubble-strewn hillside toward the pair. A glance at the young woman told Julie she was dead. The man, stretched out not far from the woman's side stirred, however.

"He's unconscious," Julie pointed out matter-of-factly, "but his breathing seems normal. Looks like he took a bad blow on the side of his head. You seem to know these people . . . who are they? And Cindy, your voice . . . I still don't understand what this is all about . . . how you knew about this accident."

Cindy's eyes were calm now, her face serene. "This is Ralph," she said, and, pointing to the girl, "that's Cathy. Take care of them for me." She slumped over and collapsed in a heap on the ground. Julie slipped over by her side, taking her head in her hands.

Shortly, Cindy's eyelids fluttered and her eyes opened. "Julie," she said sleepily, "where are we? What are we doing here?" It was Cindy's own squeaky voice, the voice she had always known. Recoiling in shock, she said. "There's been an accident. Where are the rest of the girls?"

"They're back at camp. Someone should have gone for help by now. Everything's going to be all right."

As if in confirmation of her statement, she heard the roar of a helicopter in the sky. Julie stood up, waving frantically, and sighed in relief when the aircraft moved toward them and she saw the friendly hand wave in response. While she waited for the copter to land, she took another look at the little girl. She seemed stronger now.

Cindy returned from the creek with a wet rag to place on Ralph's forehead, and Julie returned to his side when she heard him moaning. When his eyes opened, his first words were, "Ruth . . . where's my wife? Ruth—"

Julie looked over at the dead woman. "I'm sorry, Mr. Weston, she didn't make it . . . but she saved your daughter's life before she left."

Pawnee Drums

HANK HAD ALWAYS claimed a lost Pawnee burial ground was located in the Flint Hills where our Scout troop camped several times a year. Grizzled, leathery-faced Hank had been a Scoutmaster since before most of our parents were born, and over the years he had earned a reputation as a teller of tall tales. When it came to the outdoors, Hank knew his stuff all right but he was not beyond stretching the truth a little to make things a little more interesting.

It was in the summer of 1956; I was thirteen then. The troop was camped at our favorite Flint Hills site. The campfire had burned down to a bed of red-hot coals that cast an orange glow against the night's blackness. For the benefit of some of the troop Tenderfeet, Hank had just related the story of the Pawnee burial grounds, noting casually, but meaningfully, that some of its occupants had been known to roam the area around the campsite. He also admonished the boys to listen carefully for the sound of the soft, rhythmic tom-tom beats that were often heard after dark on hot, still nights. Some of the younger boys looked wide-eyed and apprehensively over their shoulders, and someone tossed a few logs on the embers to rekindle the campfire's flame.

Hank sat near the fire, surrounded now by some of the boys who had edged their way closer as he, in his own imperturbably sober way, had offered a few ghostly tales from his vast repertoire. He himself looked like a solemn old medicine man as the fire cast eerie shadows on his bronzed face.

I was full of the cockiness of a boy embarking on his teens that summer and was a bit contemptuous of what I saw as adult pomposity. Somebody ought to take the old boy down a notch, I thought. I nudged my best friend, Harvey Willits, and nodded toward Hank.

"Hey, Hank," I said, "you're always talking about that old Pawnee burial ground whenever we come out here. How come you've never shown us where it's at?"

Unfazed, Hank drawled matter-of-factly, "I told you, the place is haunted. Now, your folks are trusting me to look out for all of you boys, and I'm not about to take you to a place like that."

"Now, come on, Hank," I said. "You can come up with a better answer than that." Harvey and some of my friends giggled, but Hank shot me a peculiar, almost hurt, look that told me I had better stop right there.

My sleep was fitful that night which was highly unusual for me, because I had always found sleep in the outdoors to be easy and deep. It was not all that hot, and I was clad only in my jockey shorts, but it seemed like I was waking up about every half hour or so and each time my back and chest were sweat-soaked, the back of my neck moist and clammy.

Finally, about two o'clock, I awoke and crawled out of my sleeping bag. It was lighter now, the stars having broken through the cloud cover that had darkened the hills the night before.

Suddenly, I jerked upright at the sound of a soft, steady, drum-like sound, apparently coming from the little valley southwest of the camp. My eyes darted around the campsite to see if anyone else had been awakened by the sound, but the camp was deathly quiet and apparently no one else had been disturbed by the noise.

Hank was sound asleep off to the far edge of the camp under a gnarled oak tree. My first instinct was to dash over and awaken him, but I remembered my skepticism of the night before and thought better of it.

The drumming was becoming noticeably louder, rising in a crescendo like the soundtrack of some African movie. Everyone else in the camp appeared to be unaware of the terrible racket. I pulled on my dirty blue jeans and slipped into the buckskin moccasins I always wore around camp, and found myself walking down the grassy slope away from camp toward the valley that lay less than a mile away. In spite of my outward bravado, I was not ordinarily one who would have wandered away, but for some unexplainable reason, I was serenely calm and unafraid as I drew nearer to the rumbling drums.

Shortly, I stepped out onto a flat, open meadow, and my eyes were drawn immediately to the brilliant, shimmering light radiating from a small area at the far end. As I walked across the meadow, I could make out the outlines of the crude pole platforms upon which rested the Indian dead: women, children, and warriors. The entire area was lit up like a football field, but the source of light was not evident. The drummer was the only animate thing in the burial ground, seated cross-legged near the center, hunched over the tom-tom in front of him, surrounded by the earthly remains of his tribesmen who had joined the Great Spirit.

Still unafraid, I entered the burial ground and approached the tom-tom beater. I stepped directly in front of him and the drumming stopped. The man remained bent over the tom-tom, however, his eyes fixed to the earth. Perspiration glistened on his narrow, bony shoulders; a single feather was anchored in his snow-white hair. Then slowly he lifted his head to meet my gaze.

"You have come," he said softly in precise English.

The old man was an emaciated version of Hank. His dark eyes, craggy nose, and angular jaw unmistakably those of our gentle Scoutmaster. But the Indian was too ancient, too withered, to be my leader.

"Yes, I have come." I said.

"You did not believe," said the old man.

"No. I did not believe," I admitted.

"Your name is Jeffrey," he said. "I am known as He Who Walks."

"Why did you call me here?" I asked.

"I am looking for my son," said the drummer. "He died in a battle with the Sioux many moons ago. He was a great warrior and killed many of our ancient enemy before he died, but his Pawnee brothers were unable to recover his body and return it to our people for burial appropriate to his great station. I have searched many moons for the remains of my fallen son so that I might return them to join his family in this place."

"I am sorry," I said.

The old Indian nodded his head solemnly. "Now go," he said, "I must join my people soon. May the Great Spirit walk with you."

"Good bye," I stammered and walked away quickly.

Reaching the foothills again, I took one last look back at the luminous burial grounds. Abruptly, the light disappeared like a television screen just turned off, leaving only the empty, grassy meadow.

When I rushed breathlessly back into camp some minutes later, I spotted Hank sitting on top of his bedroll, his back leaning against the oak, calmly puffing on his long-stemmed pipe. I moved over to him, taking a place at his side.

"I noticed you were gone," he said quietly. "Have trouble sleeping tonight?"

I nodded my head affirmatively. "Hank," I said, "that Pawnee burial ground is down there in the valley, isn't it? At the south end of the meadow."

Hank's eyes softened. He wasn't one to talk much, but his eyes always told you when he understood. "Yes. It's down there, Jeff. So you found it, huh?"

"Uh huh."

"Only a few have ever been privileged to see it," he said mysteriously.

"Hank," I asked, "do you have a son?"

"I had a son," he said. Traces of moisture gathered at the corners of his eyes. "He was lost in action in World War II. It was during the Normandy Invasion. They never identified his body. We were never able to bring him home; we don't even know where he was buried." He wrapped his thick arm around my shoulders, "But don't concern yourself about it, Jeff. I've had a good life. In a way, the boys of this troop are all my sons, and in a lot of cases, I've had more impact on the lives of the boys of this troop than their own fathers have. Yes, in some ways, I suppose I've found my own son right here in this troop."

I learned a lot about what made Hank tick that night.

Ron Schwab

The River's Call

"I WANT TO warn each of you to stay away from the river after dark, and after everyone is sacked in for the night, I would strongly suggest that you do not go outside the camp area. There is a legend about this river, and whether you believe in ghosts or not, there is no reason to take unnecessary chances." Those were the words of the guide who was leading our church youth group on a canoe trip down the Big Blue River.

According to the legend, there was a beautiful young Indian maiden called Spring Bird who lived in a Pawnee village not far from here. She and a warrior called Elk Man were very much in love and planned to be married.

A week before their marriage was to occur, Elk Man was killed in battle with the Sioux. When the war party returned to the village leading Elk Man's rider-less pony, Spring Bird was so overcome by grief she ran hysterically from the village. Her father followed her to a bluff that overlooked the river and found her standing there, and when he called to her, she turned toward him with out-stretched arms. As he moved to console her in her grief, the little bluff began to cave away. He rushed to grasp her hands and pull her to safety, but she was carried into the river beneath toms of rock and dirt.

As the years went by, warriors of the tribe and even white settlers, some of whom were supposed to be extremely strong swimmers, drowned mysteriously in the river. Some members of the tribe insisted they had seen Spring Bird strolling in the woods along the river before several of the tragic accidents, and one small boy even claimed to have seen the maiden lead one unfortunate victim over the bank's edge.

Some twenty years after Spring Bird's death, one young tribesman maintained he was walking in the woods one evening when he encountered a young Pawnee maiden whom he had never seen in the village before. The young man described her as the most beautiful young woman he had ever seen, and according to elders in the tribe, his description of her conformed to that of Spring Bird in every detail.

The young woman was flirtatious and charming, and he was totally smitten by her. She invited him to come with her to the river to enjoy the lovely view and he went with her willingly. As they neared the river, he caught sight of a friend fishing on the bank's edge and called a greeting to him. When he turned, the young woman was gone, leaving no sign she had ever existed.

The tribe's medicine man told the youthful warrior he was indeed fortunate; the maiden had doubtless been Spring Bird and she would have led him to certain death in the deep, swift current of the river.

The guide told us that the story of Spring Bird's ghost is only a legend, and, if Spring Bird's lost spirit does wander thought the woods, her magic spell was probably no more than that any young woman is able to cast over a young man. Nevertheless, he warned us again to stay close to camp and, under no circumstances to go near the river.

The Friendly Face

THE MAN'S FACE was not deformed or grotesque—not even ugly, for that matter. But every time Karen thought of the face, shivers raced down her spine and she broke out in a cold sweat. Rugged, Germanesque features characterized the face. She was struck especially by the firm-set jaw line and deep-set eyes sheltered by thick, dark eyebrows. The long sharp nose seemed out of place on the full, rounded face and gave it a rather solemn quality in spite of the pleasant smile that seemed to be perpetually engraved there. There was really nothing about the face, she reminded herself, that should frighten her . . . but it did.

Without fail, every night for a month now, the face had visited Karen Nelson in her dreams. It was a face without a body —or without a head, for that matter—more like a Halloween mask floating in the air, suspended on some invisible strings. But unlike a mask, it spoke to her, always delivering the same message in the same breathy, whispering voice, "I have missed you so much, Karen. Please come visit me soon."

She would always awaken at this point, her eyes peering just above the sheets to investigate her bedroom for reassurance that indeed she was alone in the room. After the second appearance of the face, her bedside lamp had been left on when she closed her eyes to seek the sleep that was now so long coming.

Maybe the face would not visit her here. The plane would be landing in Denver soon. She would be met at the airport by a van that would take her to Camp Rosewood in the heart of the Rocky Mountains.

She looked forward to the summer at Rosewood. She had never been there before, but she had been spending most of her summers at one camp or another since she was eight years old. Homesickness would not be a problem. Karen's mother always had other plans for her own summer, but Karen didn't mind; she hardly knew her mother, Trudy Nelson.

Her mother was wealthy, she knew that, evidently the beneficiary of a substantial inheritance from Karen's grandfather. Trudy Nelson's financial circumstances enabled her to send Karen to private boarding schools during the school term and to camp during the summer.

The month she had recently spent in her mother's stately mansion was the longest visit she had in the home since she was five years old, and the face had come to visit her the first night she was there. Of course, Trudy had been in Europe during this time, and Karen had been left in the care of the family servants.

At least she knew who her mother was. That was more than she could say about her father. Oh, yes, his name was Richard Nelson, but he had left Trudy when Karen was less than a year old, and Trudy had apparently taken great pains to destroy every shred of evidence that he had ever existed. Karen had not seen so much as a photograph of her father and knew virtually nothing of his background except that, according to Trudy's version, he was a vicious, evil man.

For most of her life, she had accepted her mother's judgment at face value, but now, as she approached young womanhood herself, Karen suspected there might be another side of the story. Perhaps her father had a good reason for absenting himself these many years.

That night after arrival at Rosewood, Karen lay awake in her bunk struggling against the sleep that was trying to overtake her, feeling with certainty that the face would visit again if she succumbed. In the stillness of the one-room cabin, the breathing of her three cabin mates, all in deep slumber, reminded Karen of the irritating hum of a vacuum cleaner. The soft hoot of an owl drifted through a window screen near her bedside and called her to the more soothing, pacifying sounds of the outdoors.

She rose from her bunk and, pulling a terry cloth robe over her flannel pajamas, stepped out into the cool night air. Her attention was drawn to girlish laughter and giggling coming from one of the cabins down the trail, and she padded barefoot down the dusty path toward the noise, hoping to find some companions who were not yet ready to surrender to exhaustion.

But as she neared the other cabin, a huge figure loomed seemingly from nowhere and stepped into her path. It was a man, a large, big-boned man with muscular arms. She shrank back, startled, and looked up to see the friendly face of her dreams, this time attached to a head and a human form.

"I have missed you so much, Karen," the man said. "I am pleased you answered my call." He extended his hand and, helplessly, she received it, acutely aware of its roughness as his fingers closed tight around her own. "Come with me, Karen," the man said.

"No," Karen whimpered, "please . . . no." She tried to scream but the words choked in her throat and the man held on with a vice-like grip. She followed him obediently away from Rosewood through the endless maze of gullies and draws that sliced through the shale-covered slopes surrounding the camp.

Much later, they walked out onto a winding, one-lane road partially grown over by grass and weeds. As the man pulled her firmly, but gently, down the steep incline, she stumbled, falling to the ground, scraping her knee. For the first time she became aware of the pain where the rock and shale had gouged and bruised her bare feet and ankles.

"I can't go any further," she said, ". . . my feet." She thought she detected a softening in the big man's deep-set eyes.

"I'll carry you," he said, "it isn't far."

Lifting her gently in his arms, the big man carried Karen down the deserted road. Karen, exhausted and frightened, slipped into semi-consciousness.

Later, she was awakened rudely by the creaking of metal against metal, her eyes opened to the macabre scene of an old, long-forgotten cemetery. She screamed and struggled to break free from the man's arms, but they tightened around her and held her close.

"Hush, child," he said, "you will not be harmed."

The iron gate clanged shut behind them and the man's feet made a swishing sound as they shuffled through the tall grass that almost hid many of the shorter granite markers that decorated the hillside.

Soon he stopped, placing Karen on the ground with her back leaning against one of the newer stone monuments, one with a rounded top.

"Please," Karen sobbed, "let me go. I don't like this place.

Please let me go back to camp. I won't tell anybody."

"I am your father, Karen," he said. "I have been calling for you, and you have answered my call."

She lifted her eyes to the man's face. She saw no malice there, only sadness, perhaps tenderness. "How do I know you're my father?" she stammered. "And how did you call me? I don't understand."

"I was never able to tell you how much I cared, Karen," he said. "I could not rest until you knew. I want you to understand that I did not want to leave you. I was a common laborer when I married your mother. For a time, she was apparently fascinated by my physical strength and unsophisticated manner; perhaps I was a novelty. But soon she tired of me, like a child with a new toy. I did not fit into her society and I was a burden on her social life, an embarrassment she felt impelled to explain to her friends. After you were born, she told me these things, and said she planned to file for divorce; she ordered me to leave the house. I loved you, Karen. You were a beautiful baby, and it broke my heart to leave you. I came out here and found work with a mining company in a now-deserted town not far from here. I intended to return and try to obtain custody of you. Realizing my chances of success were poor, I planned to find work near your mother's home so we could be together from time to time. But a mining accident intervened and I was unable to return. Now, I only want you to be secure in the knowledge that you had a father who loved you."

Tears streaked Karen's cheeks. She jumped up, "You are my father . . . I know it. Oh, I'm so glad you found me." She reached out to hug the kindly man, but her arms encircled only empty space and she fell again to the ground. The man was gone.

Almost before her eyes he had disintegrated into nothingness. "Father," she called, "where are you? We have so much to talk about. Father! Father!" She lay there on the ground, hiding her face in her arms, sobbing uncontrollably and hysterically until, insensitive to the chilling air, she surrendered to deep sleep.

She awoke at first light to the summer chorus of the mountain birds. It was strange, she thought, how daylight transformed the little cemetery into almost a happy place. Now she knew no fear.

But what about the man and the events of the night before? Was it all a dream? Had she been walking in her sleep and somehow wandered by accident to this place? She rose, brushing the dust and grass from her robe, when out of the corners of her eyes she saw the inscription on the tombstone she had leaned against the night before: Richard Nelson . . . birth date unknown . . . died July 8, 2000. The date was only a few months after her father would have left home. She touched the stone gently then turned and headed toward the road, confident she would find her way back to camp. The face would haunt her no more.

The Claw

EVERYONE HAS HEARD of Big Foot, the Abominable Snowman, and others in the cast of legendary creatures. It seems that every part of the world has some type of monster-creature that cultivates the imaginations of its inhabitants. There are some who will swear to having seen such creatures, and there has been substantial photographic and other evidence supporting existence of the legendary subject on occasion. Of course, some will insist that the monsters are the product of tall tales or even a hoax.

Our own county is the home of such a creature. He had been dubbed "The Claw" by those who have studied his habits. We first became aware of his existence a few years back. The sheriff's department had been called upon to investigate a number of strange animal deaths and mutilations, mostly cattle and hogs. In every instance, the unfortunate animal had its belly slashed open and its entrails removed. In all other respects, the carcass was undisturbed, and the farmers of the area were incensed at the senseless killing. Coyotes, bobcats and other wild creatures would at least devour the prey.

At first, it was thought that the killings were the result of teenage pranks or the work of some deranged cult, but the investigators were soon convinced otherwise.

Early one morning, the sheriff was called out to the Bauer farm a mile or so north of Borderview. There he was shown a prize bull that had been killed and disemboweled in the same manner as the other animals. There had been a light rain the night before, however, and this time there were tracks to follow. The sheriff and his two deputies agreed they had to be the tracks of a giant bear, perhaps a grizzly, although they had never known any bears to inhabit this part of the state or anywhere else in Nebraska, for that matter.

Armed with high-powered rifles and accompanied by a pair of good coon hounds, they headed along the wooded river bottom where the tracks led. The dogs ranged far ahead, and from their howling, the men knew they were on the trail of something. In a short while, they lost sight of the dogs, but soon they heard the frantic barking and baying of the hounds and then their terrifying cries of pain as they engaged in some ferocious battle in the distance. Above the howling, they could hear the loud grunting, growling noise, not unlike the sound that might come from a wounded bear.

In a few moments, the howling of the dogs stopped and there was only an ominous silence. The men quickened their pace and charged breathlessly over a ridge to come face to face with the murderer, two grotesquely mutilated dogs at his feet. Standing on two legs like a primate, it was a hairy, bear-like creature, close to eight feet tall. Its face was more like that of an ape or a man, but the appendages at the end of its powerful arms were what shocked the onlookers most. It had neither hands nor paws, only a single, giant claw, shaped something like a bear claw, but as long and sharp as a hunting knife, emerging from the end of each arm.

The creature lurched menacingly toward the men, but suddenly turned and lumbered off into the woods, leaving them frozen in their tracks. What the sheriff and his deputies had seen apparently dampened their enthusiasm for the hunt, and they made no attempt to follow.

After they related their tale to the press, the sheriff and his deputies became the laughing stock of the county, and soon after, all three resigned and moved away from the community.

Since that time, however, other sightings of The Claw have been reported from time to time, and every few years it seems like there is a streak of the otherwise unexplainable killings.

The Hazing

MORGAN MANSION SAT on the outskirts of town, almost hidden by the towering trees and tangled undergrowth that surrounded it. When I last saw the old frame house, the stone foundation was beginning to crumble and the weathered, two-story structure above was starting to sag and lean. I suspect it has been razed by now and leveled to the ground. Whatever its fate, I have no desire to return to the site of the old mansion to find out.

According to local legend in the small town where I attended college, the huge, castle-like structure had once been the gracious home of the community's most prominent family, and, in its day, had been the hub of social life for most of the town's elite. The home's builder was dynamic, ambitious Albert Morgan who harbored visions of a family dynasty, but, unfortunately, his line was doomed to die out. Neither his daughter, Gertrude Morgan, nor his son, Arnold Morgan, chose to marry, and, after the death of their parents, resided together in the stately mansion, presiding over the decline and demise of the Morgan empire and the mansion that symbolized it. The depression of the 1930s brought the final disintegration of the Morgan fortune. Although Arnold and Gertrude had apparently preserved

Ron Schwab

sufficient resources to maintain themselves in relatively humble style, the two withdrew entirely from the community's social scene, and, over a period of several years, became complete recluses, seen only on rare occasions by the grocery delivery boys and other persons who provided their essential services.

Those who saw Arnold said he was prone to leap into long tirades and sermons about the drunks, indigents, and other parasites of society who should be destroyed and eradicated from the earth. Although in his sixties at the time, it was reported that he seemed in excellent physical condition, his lean, upright body belying the age evidenced by his white, flowing mane and creased, craggy face. His eyes allegedly flashed with fire and brimstone when he launched into one of his angry sermons. The children of the community soon tagged him with the nickname, Crazy Arnold.

Gertrude, on the other hand, was a tiny, spindly woman, a few years her brother's senior. She was quiet and demure, seemingly a kindly woman, who had some reputation for offering a meal or refreshments to any wayward soul who might come to the mansion's kitchen door. More than once, some hungry tramp had been referred to the Morgan kitchen.

One dry August day, a frightened, hysterical tramp, exhibiting a ghastly, raw rope burn on his neck, showed up at the local police station. According to the vagrant, Arnold Morgan had overpowered him at the Morgan kitchen table while Gertrude was serving him a meal. The brother and sister had bound his hands behind his back and taken him upstairs to a room they called the execution chamber, where he was greeted by a thick noose suspended from a heavy beam. Arnold had forced the man to stand on a chair, while Gertrude placed the noose

86

around his neck. When Arnold had kicked the chair out from under the vagrant, however, the man somehow wedged his head free from the noose and tumbled to the floor. He had thrown his shoulder into Arnold's chest, leaving the old man gasping on the floor while he made his way awkwardly down the stairs and out the door.

A short time later, when the police entered Morgan Mansion with a search warrant, they found Gertrude and Crazy Arnold hanging side by side from the beam in the execution chamber. Apparently anticipating the investigation that would surely follow the vagrant's escape, they had chosen to take their own lives.

In the days that followed, more than a dozen bodies were exhumed from the grounds around the house. The house was closed up by the next of kin and efforts to sell it were fruitless. Some in the community maintained it was haunted and that fluorescent-like outlines of Arnold and Gertrude could be seen through the dusty windows at night.

The guys in our fraternity had all heard the story of Morgan Mansion, and I suggested that the place would be a perfect setting for initiating the pledge class of 1993. The idea had unanimous support, so the night of our fraternity initiation, after relating the story of Morgan Mansion to the pledges, we led them through the iron gates of the deserted estate. In order to pass the test, it was required that the pledges enter the house one at a time, climb the stairway to the second story, go to the window and wave acknowledgment to the fraternity members who would be waiting outside.

The first pledge to enter the house did not make it to the second floor. Not more than ten minutes after he climbed through the basement window and started his journey up the stairs, he crashed through the main floor window screaming in terror. After calming him down, we gathered from his babblings that he had heard some ghostly moaning from the upstairs room, and then had seem some gaseous, transparent figure at the top of the stairs with a rope in his hand.

We laughed uproariously at the young man's display of imagination, but two of the other pledges did not. They turned and raced down the path toward the gate before anyone could stop them.

That left Charles Weatherby who was apparently not frightened by his fellow pledge's story. Weatherby picked up a solid hickory stick and clutched it tightly in his hand. "I don't know who you guys put in there," he said, "but he's going to get a surprise if he makes a move for me." He laughed contemptuously at our insistence that we had not planted anyone in the house.

The other pledge begged Weatherby not to enter the house and then implored us to stop him. But Weatherby marched bravely up to the open basement window and crawled in without a moment's hesitation.

Ten minutes passed; then twenty, and finally, a half hour. Weatherby should have made it to the window easily in ten minutes time. Now we began to feel uneasy; perhaps he had fallen somewhere and was injured. Could some dangerous maniac be occupying the house? Perhaps a tramp who had taken up residency there?

Then we saw the light at the designated window. No, it was the glowing outline of an old man. Was that a rope suspended in his hand? Then it disappeared as quickly as it had come. We looked at each other in astonishment and disbelief; no one said a word and no one moved.

The huge front door of the mansion creaked slowly open and a white-haired man staggered out onto the porch and down the warped, wooden steps. Someone or something closed the doors, which had been locked earlier, behind him. The figure started toward us and I moved to lead the exodus from the grounds, when I realized the man was wearing Charlie Weatherby's clothes.

"Wait a moment," I whispered to the others.

As the form approached, I knew it was Weatherby, but his face was pale and his eyes totally expressionless as they stared straight ahead, almost unseeing. His hair, formerly coal black, had turned white as newly fallen snow.

"Charlie," I said, "what happened?" But he did not seem to hear. His lips moved but he only jabbered some unintelligible animal-like sounds.

"Look at his neck," said one of the guys. Droplets of blood oozed from the tender flesh around his neck where the raw, red outline of a rope had left its mark.

We never did find out what happened to Charlie Weatherby that night. He was hospitalized for a time, but the abrasions on his neck were only superficial, and had not precipitated the damage to his mind. Charlie Weatherby was institutionalized in an asylum and remains there to this day.

For me, the experience scarred my life. I shudder to think of the unforeseen consequences that can result from the hazing and harassment we perform in the name of initiations in our society. And I refuse to tamper with anything that even hints of the supernatural.

Coyote Woman

THERE IS A Pawnee burial ground several miles south of Rose Creek. Most of the remains buried there are those of a medicine band that was massacred by a Sioux war party one crisp fall evening just before dusk.

Medicine band was a term often used in referring to a small group of medicine men, their novices and family members who lived and traveled together much of each year, visiting other villages from time to time to minister to their spiritual and medical needs. Most prominent of this band was the only Pawnee medicine woman, or shaman, called Coyote Woman.

On the night of the raid, the Sioux took Coyote Woman's ten-year-old daughter, White Fox, captive along with several other Pawnee children, and as they raced off under the cover of descending darkness, Coyote Woman chased after the Sioux ponies on foot. It was a fruitless effort. An hour later she returned to her village and helped the few surviving members prepare their tribesmen for burial.

That task completed, she refused to leave the burial site and ordered the others to go on, declaring that she would remain behind to await the return of White Fox.

She sat down and shrieked and cried and sang the death songs. It was said that her crying and singing were heard many miles away for nearly a month. One passing Pawnee reported that he saw her sitting in the middle of the burial ground, evidently eating nothing, starving herself and wasting away.

What became of Coyote Woman, no one knows, but over the years, the Pawnee and later, the white settlers, reported that for a month or so every fall, coyotes would be heard howling nightly from the direction of the burial ground and later in the full darkness of night, the soft beat of tom-toms would spread over the hills. Some reported from time to time seeing a slender Indian woman walking quietly along the deer trails that crisscrossed the rough landscape. She was often heard chanting softly, and it was speculated that this might be Coyote Woman seeking her lost child.

On at least three occasions over the years, small children, all daughters, were reported missing and never found. In one instance, a small boy who shared a room with his sister claimed that an Indian woman had entered their room at night and she had glowing red eyes and he had watched her paralyzed by fear. The woman gently shook his sister from her sleep, and he said his sister met the woman's eyes as if she were hypnotized and she rose from her bed in a trance and simply followed the woman out the door and into the surrounding woods. By the time he had recovered his wits and awakened his parents, there was no sign of the girl.

Coyote Woman stories continue to this day. Often the coyotes can be heard on brisk, fall evenings and many have asserted that the soft beat of the tom-toms from the burial ground can be heard more often than not during the fall of year, and this is when Coyote Woman is said to begin her wanderings and visits, seeking a replacement for her lost child.

McDowell's Tomb

ABOUT FIVE MILES south of Fairbury, Nebraska is a place called McDowell's Tomb. The land on which the tomb is located is part of the state park system now, and the place is rich with history—some fact, some legend, and part, I have no doubt, just outright fiction. I can only tell you what I know and relate my own experience with the tomb.

John McDowell was an early settler of Jefferson County. He lived in Fairbury but owned a small parcel of land along the banks of Rose Creek. He was a strange man, a loner, and no one knew much about him except that he was determined to be buried on the plot of ground he owned. In fact, McDowell decided to construct his own tomb and over a period of some ten years, he walked the distance to his land, sometimes making the trip daily, and others camping there for several days at a time. With shovel and pick axe, he dug a cave into a sandstone wall that loomed above Rose Creek.

Early in the venture, a few of McDowell's city neighbors took pity on him and offered to help McDowell with the project. They didn't stay long, though, because the place was snake-infested. They reported that dozens of snakes were coiled in the work place. It was as if they were curious about this gnarled, bearded white-haired man and the project he had undertaken. The neighbors said that McDowell even had names for many of the snakes and spoke to them as he worked.

Anyway, the company McDowell kept assured that his effort would be a solitary one. Over the years, McDowell finally completed his tomb, or mausoleum, as some call it. When it was finished, he had carved out a huge room in the sandstone, and on one wall was a ledge where his coffin was supposed to rest.

The work finished, McDowell wrote out specific instructions regarding his burial in the tomb and paid the local undertaker in advance to see that his wishes were carried out. He also left instructions in his will to his two nephews directing them to have his casket placed in the tomb and to install a steel gate there to keep out unwelcome visitors.

A few weeks later, McDowell died. The nephews, however, resisted carrying out their uncle's instructions as they didn't want the embarrassment of having their uncle resting in the homemade tomb. The undertaker tried to carry out his customer's wishes, but the nephews got a court order stopping him since they were the executors of their uncle's estate and the ultimate heirs to the land.

Finally, after several weeks of squabbling, McDowell was laid to rest in the Fairbury cemetery.

For years, McDowell's vacant tomb was visited by hikers and curiosity seekers, although many were deterred by the reptiles that always seemed to congregate. Neighbors claimed that on quiet summer evenings you could hear a shovel clanging against stone coming from the direction of the tomb. Nobody ever bothered to check it out, however.

My last experience with the cave came when I was about fifteen years old. Our Boy Scout troop used to camp along Rose Creek about half a mile from the tomb, and some days we would hike over to the cave to explore. For some reason, though, not long after we got there, snakes—bull snakes, garter snakes, even an occasional prairie rattler—would start to show up and they never seemed to be afraid of us like snakes usually were. About this time, we always moved out pretty fast.

That summer we were camping at our usual site up the creek from the cave. It was nearly midnight and pitch black when a dozen of us were sitting around the dying campfire, listening to the college-age son of our Scout leader spin ghost stories and tall tales. He was an intelligent, basically decent young man, but was a bit cocky and arrogant after having spent his first year at the university. He suddenly had the inspiration that he wanted to take the group on a hike to the tomb. I wasn't about to go, but Ted, the leader's son, finally needled and dared one of the seventeen-year-olds to go with him. They took off and the rest of us tossed a little more wood on the fire and waited silently.

About a half hour later, we heard a blood-curdling scream coming from the area of the tomb. Our Scout leader came out of his tent like a bolt. "What was that?" he asked.

"Ted and Ralph went to the tomb," I replied.

"Oh," he chuckled. "Ted's just trying to scare everybody."

We all waited. Moments later, Ralph entered the camp, his eyes round and his lips trembling, his face white as a sheet. Shortly, he was followed by Ted, although we didn't recognize him at first. Ted's dark hair had turned white as snow, his eyes were glazed over, and when he tried to talk words wouldn't come out of his mouth. While our leader tried to bring Ted to his senses, Ralph related the story.

As they approached the cave, he said they could see a shimmering white light coming from its depth. They assumed someone else was exploring the cave and they crept closer. Hearing nothing, they called out and got no response. They climbed the slope to the mouth of the tomb and entered. There on the shelf where McDowell's coffin was to have been placed, lay a scrawny old man with long white hair and a scraggly beard. The space around him glowed like radioactivity.

Ted took a few steps toward him and said, "Hey, old man." The man's head turned, and where his eyes should have been were deep, empty sockets. Ralph turned to run, but Ted was frozen in his place. Suddenly, snakes began to emerge from the cave walls, dropping from the ceiling onto the young man's head and shoulders. It was Ralph's scream we had heard; Ted was mute, frozen in place. Ralph grabbed his arm and jerked him away, sweeping off the snakes with his other hand. Obediently, Ted had followed him, shivering and speechless. Ralph had seen our campfire and raced toward it, weaving through the trees and brush with Ted not far behind.

We didn't go to investigate. We packed up our gear that night. Ted never really did recover entirely. He spent a year in a mental institution. He never did return to college. He went to work as a bookkeeper in his father's company, never married and never socialized, and, to my knowledge, never spoke of what happened that night.

The Uninvited Guest

My wife, Bev, has—or had—a penchant for fixing up old houses, and for some years this had us moving like nomads from home to home. Bev would spot a decaying, neglected house calling for her tender touch, and a few weeks later our current abode would be on the market, and, within a month or two, we would be carting our furniture and personal belongings into a dilapidated house. Bev would go to work with sledge hammer and saw while we lived among clutter and dust, and she, with only occasional grumbling contributions from me, would truly transform the proverbial sow's ear into a silk purse. We inevitably ended up with a lovely restored and unique home . . . and, of course, it was time to move on again.

On a brisk October day some years ago we settled into Bev's latest rescue project, a two-story monstrosity adjacent to our previous residence that only Bev could love. As a matter of fact, the previous owner was planning to bulldoze it down when Bev intervened to save the dying house, which she, unknown to me, had her eye on ever since we moved next door. The house was as near hopeless as any we had lived in, but Bev and I, along with our two cats, Bennie and Punkin, once again embarked on a new adventure among the rubble of our new home.

I was comforted by the knowledge that by spring the house would be livable and by another spring it would be quite elegant. The cats obviously did not share my sentiments. Normally trusting, affectionate lap cats, they turned hyperactive and spooky, often hiding under the bed and couch, emerging only when Bev and I were both in the room. Bedtimes were horrendous. We always put our cats in the basement at night, and, with the promise of a special snack, Punkin, a plump, little calico fur ball, and Bennie, a rangy black and white shorthair, would obediently trot to their nighttime quarters at the sound of the treat bag rattling. Not so in the "new" house. Here they fought bedtime like infants, running and hiding and yowling mournfully when we captured them and put them to bed at night. Our bedroom was on the second floor, but we could hear the cats crying during the night, and, in the morning, they would charge frantically into the kitchen when Bev opened the basement door. Their behavior was a mystery.

Our first task whenever Bev and I nest in a new house is to carve out a den or study, where we each have some workspace and our separate computers. Being addicted to books, I always install some shelving to store the most treasured of my library, while harboring a dream that someday we can have the room to reunite all of the books in a single place. We fashioned a small study of calm and quiet here, and when Bev was not working on a house project and I was not working late at my law office, we savored those moments in the study reading, writing, or surfing the Internet while Bennie snoozed on my desk, and Punkin purred at Bev's feet. It was one such night a month after we had moved into the house that we were ensconced in the study.

Suddenly, both cats rose up and began to growl, their hair standing on their backs, their eyes fixed on the doorway. Chills raced down my own spine. The room had turned cold as a meat locker.

"What's the matter with them?" Bev asked.

"I don't know. They must have heard something . . . maybe a mouse."

"It's freezing in here," Bev said.

"I'll turn up the thermostat," I said as I got up and stepped slowly and just a little cautiously toward the empty hallway. Instantly the chill evaporated, and the cats stopped growling. Later, at bedtime, we had a marathon cat chase, and gentle Punkin even nipped me before I plopped her down on the basement landing.

This scene was replayed three or four times a week over the next month, and Bev and I were starting to get as uneasy as the cats about the episodes. Then one night, as we were sleeping, the bedroom door opened. I heard the creaking and sat up, my heart skipping several beats. For a moment I thought I saw a woman in a long gown standing there, but I blinked my eyes and the doorway was suddenly empty. Again, the room turned frigid.

Bev awakened. "What is it?"

The door closed. The room warmed. "I don't know, but I don't like it."

I didn't sleep again that night.

The next day I decided to put my research training to work. I was more than curious. I was scared. I didn't know if I'd ever get a good night's sleep in that house again. I made a visit to the register of deeds office and checked the deed records. Based upon a mortgage filed against the property, I concluded the house had been built in 1881, about 120 years previous, by Cyrus and Ida Musgrove. They had owned the property about ten years before it was sold at a tax foreclosure sale. After that the house had changed hands thirty or more times. This was unheard of in a town of 4,000 or so people. It would not be unusual for a residence to be transferred only half a dozen times in that period.

That evening I called on Frank Soloman, a crotchety old guy who lived four houses down the block. Frank didn't get along with most of the neighbors, but he never seemed to mind me much, and, in fact, if I said so much as a "hello" to him as I walked past his home, he would corral me and talk my ear off. When Frank answered the phone, I identified myself and asked him if he knew any of the people that had lived in the house over the years.

"Lived in this neighborhood over 50 years, but nobody ever stayed in the Musgrove house long enough for me to get acquainted too good."

"Musgrove house?"

"Yeah. They say some folks named Musgrove built the place back before the 1900s. Then they just disappeared one day. Left all their things behind. Place finally sold for taxes. Ever see any ghosts there?" The old devil chuckled.

"Ghosts?"

"Yep. Some folks used to say there were ghosts in the house. Ain't heard that for a while, though. But if you wanted to sell a place I don't suppose you'd brag about them kind of guests, would you?"

"I guess not, but anybody who would think a house was haunted has a bit of an overactive imagination, I think."

Frank shifted to another subject then, and I let him rattle on a spell before excusing myself. I decided not to say anything to Bev about my conversation with Frank.

A week later, after several more nighttime door openings and another eerie moment in the doorway of the study, I was working on a legal research project at my laptop with my trusty felines snuggled side by side and dozing on my desk. I could hear the clang of metal against stone in the basement where Bev was prying up old brick from a part of the floor. She planned to replace the brick with concrete in hopes of discouraging bugs and other critters from entering from the dirt and gravel bed beneath. Her vision declared that this mess would someday be a family room. Why was I not doing this physically demanding work? I am a firm believer in equal opportunity for women, especially when it comes to unpleasant jobs.

The research was making me sleepy—I have never especially enjoyed the research part of my work—and my eyes closed momentarily and I started to nod off. My slumber was aborted by hysterical screams from the basement. The cats leapt off the desk, raced for our bedroom and shot under the bed. I rushed down the stairway, fearing the worst, certain that Bev had somehow been injured. By the time I reached the basement the screaming had stopped, and I found Bev standing in a dark corner speechless and petrified, pointing at the floor. I came up next to her and stared at the moldy human skull with empty eyes and a half-toothed mouth grinning up at us.

Having no other inspiration, I called 911 and asked that someone from the sheriff's office come over. The next day, sheriff's deputies dug up the remaining bones, eventually assembling a perfect human skeleton. Forensic studies determined that the remains were those of a woman who died more than a century ago. Damage to the back of the skull suggested she might have died as a result of a devastating blow to the head. The sheriff and I surmised that Cyrus Musgrove must have murdered Ida, removed the brick, buried her, and replaced the brick . . . then beat it out of town.

I employed a contractor to replace the basement floor, receiving no protest from Bev, and she continued to work on other renovation projects. The cats calmed down and started accepting bedtime with less resistance. We got through the Christmas holidays with no more strange happenings. Neither Bev nor I acknowledged to the other that there had ever been anything supernatural in our house. We did not believe in such things—or she didn't, having a mind firmly grounded in science and reality.

New Year's Eve we celebrated as usual by staying home with plans to toast with root beer at Eastern Standard Time. We were enjoying our study that evening, indulging in some holiday nuts and popcorn while we caught up on some reading and listened to the soothing music of Floyd Cramer's piano floating from the stereo. Then it was suddenly *deja vu*. Punkin and Bennie began to emit throaty growls and crouched on their respective desktops, glaring at the vacant doorway; the room felt like we were sitting in the middle of an igloo.

Several months later we sold the house as a work in progress. We found a nice single story, ranch-style built on a slab. No basement. Bev has redecorated and done some minor remodeling, but she seems content here. She's not searching for another house to rescue. We might have found home.

The Guardian

CAN ANYONE TELL me what a guardian is? A protector. Someone who protects another person from danger or helps her when she is in trouble.

There is a legend that Camp Jefferson has a guardian who protects and looks after campers and that it is not just good luck there's never been a terrible accident or tragedy here. I've always had a particular interest in this legend because the history of it has a connection with someone in my family, and I have experienced things that lead me to think there may be some truth to it.

Some of you may have heard of a Comanche war chief named Quanah Parker. Quanah was the son of Cynthia Parker who had been captured by the Comanche as a child, and who was raised in the tribe and eventually married Quanah's father, who was also a great Comanche chief.

Quanah led the Comanche in the last days of the Indian Wars, and his was one of the last tribes to make peace. When the tribe was resettled on the reservation in Oklahoma, he used his talents as a leader to become a very successful, wealthy businessman.

Other Indians said he had great mystical powers and had dreams and visions that almost always foretold the future.

So what does Quanah Parker have to do with the legend of Camp Jefferson? We only have to go back a century and a half to when Quanah Parker was only 16 years old. Not a yet a chief, but considered a young man of great powers.

One night on the Texas prairie in a time of no rain and no buffalo, Quanah had a vision that he must go north and find a white buffalo. In the dream, Quanah was told by whispers soft as rustling leaves that he should travel north, and when he found a white buffalo, he should touch the buffalo three times with his coup stick. Under no circumstances was he to harm the buffalo or any of his herd.

After counting coup, he was to locate a river. There Quanah was to establish by natural landmarks an area that would be a sacred safe place for the white buffalo. No harm would come to the buffalo there, and no harm would come to any man, white or Indian. It would become a great council place where all men could meet to discuss their differences. The white buffalo would be the protector of the place. The voice told him that rain would return.

Quanah left his village in the spring, and traveled northward for many days across the territories we now know as Oklahoma and Kansas, moving further north than any Comanche had ever been.

One morning, as he crossed the hills of the southern part of what we now know as Jefferson County, Nebraska, the ominous rattle of a snake startled Quanah's horse and it reared and threw the young brave on the rocky slope. The horse raced away and the rattlesnake struck, biting Quanah on his ankle. Quickly, he took his knife and made slashes over the fang marks in an effort to bleed the poison from his body, but it was too late and dizziness overwhelmed him. Chills racked his body, and he broke out into a fierce sweat. Within an hour, he lost consciousness.

He lay there among the searing rocks most of the day, but as darkness descended and the evening air cooled, he awakened briefly and then fell back into his troubled sleep. Once he awakened to the snarling and growling of a pack of wolves that inched ever closer, but he was too weak to fend them off. Then suddenly, a huge white figure loomed from the darkness and charged the wolves. It struck one wolf that raced away yelping, and then wheeled to face the others. Some of the braver wolves attacked, but were no match for the beast's sharp horns. They quickly retreated into the night to look for easier prey.

Throughout the night, Quanah would awaken from time to time, and shortly before sunrise, he crawled to his coup stick which had fallen nearby. The white buffalo stood there unmoving as Quanah raised himself up and touched him three times with the stick. Quanah fell back and collapsed again on the ground. When he awoke at sunrise, the buffalo was gone and his pony grazed in the meadow at the bottom on the hill.

Later that day, Quanah made his way to what the white man later called the Little Blue River which follows the edge of Camp Jefferson. He marked a huge cottonwood tree as the corner of one boundary and found a prominent outcropping of rocks that designated another. Each location he touched three times with his coup stick and chanted and sang prayers to the Great Spirit.

The next morning, a tiny herd of perhaps twenty-five buffalo grazed within the area Quanah had marked, and the white buffalo fed on a hilltop above the others. Quanah returned home knowing in his heart that he had completed his quest. And the rains came in and the grass grew.

For many years after, other Indians and white travelers reported seeing a white buffalo in this area, but strangely, no one ever thought of killing it. For many years after the buffalo would have died, people continued to report seeing a white buffalo.

Several times over the years, campers who visited Camp Jefferson claimed to see the buffalo, although, of course, no one believed them. One young girl who fell into the pond at night insisted she was saved by a buffalo who charged into the water and allowed her to latch onto his fur while he dragged her back to shore.

My own experience was many years ago when I was at this camp with my own daughters. We warned all of the campers to stay in their cabins after they went to bed, but my daughter, Linda, did not always listen to the wisdom of her father, and she decided to take a hike in the moonlight after everyone was supposed to be in bed. Later, when we checked the cabins to be sure that everyone was safe and sound, Linda's bunk was empty. We awakened the other leaders and began a search. After about an hour, I was panic-stricken. Suddenly, off to the south, I saw a glowing white light moving toward the camp. Moments later, Linda strolled out of the trees. She was frightened and in tears from being lost. I asked her how she found her way back.

"The buffalo brought me," she said. "The white buffalo."

I shivered involuntarily and I saw the white light moving away from the camp grounds. My curiosity got the best of me and I chased after it. I followed the light into a clearing and then suddenly it disappeared. I looked down at the ground, and the only thing with me in the clearing was an old buffalo skull.

I didn't know what to think. Was it Linda's sometimes-vivid imagination? Was she rescued by the white buffalo? It doesn't matter. The story had a happy ending, and it added another chapter to the legend.